CHRISTMAS AT SPINDLEWOOD

ZARA THORNE

Re-published in 2024 by Bloodhound Books.

www.bloodhoundbooks.com

Print ISBN: 978-1-917449-05-2

CHAPTER 1

Laura Engleby stood at the tall window of the turret room, her arms wrapped around herself for imaginary protection against the morning chill. The circular room with its lofty vaulted ceiling was her favourite place to sit and read, or just daydream. Overlooking the front of the house, it afforded far-reaching views of the garden, extending across the downward slope of the lawn and beyond the winding drive to the stretch of road just visible between the trees. The sky was a mass of low grey cloud. A fine mist hung over the rooftops of the village of Charnley Acre and shrouded the homely, rounded shapes of the South Downs.

Ten soft chimes sounded from the grandmother clock in the hall downstairs. And there, turning into the gated entrance of Spindlewood right on time, was the bright-green van with 'Green and Fragrant Gardening Services' painted in orange on the side. By the time Laura had abandoned her look-out point, bounded down two flights of stairs and opened the front door, the van was parked on the gravelled forecourt, the driver's door flung back.

Clayton Masters, the owner of the gardening business,

jumped down from the driver's seat and gave her a cheery 'good morning' as she approached. Saul, his young assistant, muttered a gruff greeting through the wound-down window on the passenger side. He looked half asleep.

The first time they'd come to work on the garden, over a year ago, Laura had asked which of them was which, nodding towards the sign on the van and pretending she thought those were their actual names. Clayton had played along, although he must have heard the joke a hundred times before.

'Well, he's Green, obviously, and I'm...'

'Obviously,' Laura had said, laughing.

She'd noticed the elder man's appreciative up-and-down glance at her. Unfortunately, she hadn't been able to stop herself from doing the same to him; she'd hoped he hadn't noticed. He'd been wearing what she now knew to be his work uniform: a chunky fisherman's jersey, combat trousers and a well-worn wax jacket. The jacket had been unzipped, giving a hint of a lean but solid physique. In that split second, Laura had also seen mid-brown hair, curling about his collar and ruffled by the wind into unruly waves, dark, earth-brown eyes, and a warm, winning smile.

The same smile as she saw now.

Saul slid down from the passenger seat, banged the door shut and rounded the van to stand beside Clayton.

'Is Holly back from uni?' he said, looking past Laura to gaze up at the house.

'Not yet, Saul. She'll be down at the end of term, around December the fifteenth. Or so she says.' Laura's daughter wasn't known for sticking to a plan. Basically, she would expect Holly when she saw her.

'Ah.' Saul nodded resignedly. He must have known what the answer would be, but that hadn't quelled his hopes.

Saul's devotion to Holly was ninety per cent her doing – at

least, that was Laura's guess. Her daughter had flirted unashamedly with him back in the summer, and when she'd come home from Birmingham for the October reading week, she'd spent most evenings in the Goose and Feather where the younger set of Charnley Acre, including Saul, usually hung out. The village being small and not exactly overendowed with night spots, the pub was the only option. Laura had casually questioned Holly about her relationship with Saul, purely out of motherly interest, of course. Holly had been quick – too quick – to explain that he was just a part of the group and they were all mates together, some of whom she'd known since school days. Holly had vastly underestimated the power of the village grapevine.

'Never you mind about Holly.' Clayton winked at Laura. 'The top beds could do with a tidy up. Fetch the clippers and sacks from the van and get going on that while I talk to Mrs Engleby, would you?'

'Oh, I didn't mean either of you to do any work in the garden today. There's nothing that can't wait.' Laura glanced towards the deep borders which were now a mass of drooping foliage and brown seed heads, the remains of summer. She quite liked the way they looked, but Clayton seemed determined so who was she to argue?

'He's best kept busy. Have this one on me.'

Saul was already opening the back doors of the van and tugging out a couple of green plastic sacks. 'Don't be silly. Of course I'll pay for his time,' Laura said. It wouldn't feel right to have work done for free.

'As you like.'

A flicker of something approaching amusement passed across Clayton's face as he fell into step beside Laura on the way to the house. She was puzzled for a second, and then it occurred to her that perhaps he wanted to keep Saul occupied in the garden so that he could talk to her alone. No, of course that wasn't the reason. *Where had that come from?* Annoyed with herself, she pushed the thought away.

As they reached the front door she went ahead, hurrying along the passage to the kitchen so that Clayton couldn't see her face which she suspected had gone a bit pink, and not only from the cold air.

'Tea?' She filled the kettle and switched it on without waiting for his response, keeping her back towards him.

When, eventually, she turned round, Clayton was sitting at the table, leaning back in the chair, hands behind his head. He looked settled, and very comfortable. She'd noticed that about him before, an air of confidence which wasn't overt, and all the more appealing for that. Again, her own thoughts struck her as entirely inappropriate and hugely embarrassing. What on earth was the matter with her this morning?

Passing Clayton his tea in a blue-and-white Cornishware mug, she sat at the other end of the table and set down her own mug with a firm clunk.

'Now,' she began, keeping her tone deliberately businesslike, 'what do you think of my idea?'

'Would you mind running it past me again?' Clayton leaned in to the table. 'Only I wasn't too sure... You didn't stop long the other day.'

On Tuesday morning, as Laura left the Ginger Cat Café, she'd spotted the Green and Fragrant van parked in a bay, further along the high street. Her mind buzzing with the news she'd just heard in the café, she'd nipped along and tapped on the driver's side window. Clayton and Saul had obviously been taking a break; Clayton had been nursing a plastic cup from a flask, Saul a can of Coke.

Clayton had wound down his window and offered a questioning smile. Hardly pausing for breath, Laura had rattled off her suggestion. It sounded half-baked to her own ears. Clayton's eyebrows had risen fractionally. It was true they'd become friendly since she'd employed him to sort out the garden at Spindlewood but no doubt he was friendly with all his customers. He must have wondered why she was so keen to help him out of his predicament.

As, indeed, she'd had cause to wonder herself, several times since.

She wasn't acting out of guilt, definitely not. The loss of the space to hold Charnley Acre's traditional Christmas market, and Clayton's Christmas tree sales plot along with it, was down to Spencer Jennings. Laura's boyfriend he might be, but his business decisions were nothing to do with her. In fact, he hadn't said a word to her about it. In the same way, the decision she was making now was entirely hers, and wasn't a clumsy attempt to make amends for Spencer's actions. She hoped Clayton didn't see it that way.

Needing to end the conversation in the street as fast as possible – it had started to feel just a tiny bit awkward – Laura had asked Clayton if he wouldn't mind coming to the house so that they could talk properly, and then, time and day having been settled, she'd set off briskly for the walk back home.

She'd only half expected him to turn up today, but here he was. It was too late to back down now.

'You'll want to start selling the Christmas trees in a couple of weeks, I imagine?' she said.

'Yep. I usually get started around the first week in December to cater for the people who like to get their trees up early.' He set down his mug of tea. 'What exactly have you heard?'

'That the Christmas market's had to be cancelled because the place where it's usually held has been earmarked for new housing – well, we've known that for ages – the village is pretty much alive with the news – and the property developers want access, much sooner than we'd thought.' She deliberately kept Spencer's name out of it; pointless, as Clayton knew as well as everyone else who was behind the development. And as for Laura's relationship with Spencer, that was pretty much common knowledge, too. With the eyes of the village upon them at every turn, there'd never been any point in trying to keep it secret.

The expansive square, reached by a twitten off the high street from one side and opening onto a wider road on the other, wasn't just home to the Christmas market. There was the May Day mini-fair with maypole dancing, the art club outdoor sessions, and the vegetable and flower auction once a month in summer. Once Spencer's company's plans had been made public and passed in outline – in double-quick time, it seemed – by the local planning authority, the village had been divided. One half could see the sense in affordable housing – people had to live somewhere, and the county had its targets to meet, after all. The other half fumed at having an integral part of the village destroyed in order to line the pockets of Spencer Jennings.

But Spencer himself was generally well-liked if, in some cases, a little grudgingly. It was hard not to like him. It helped his cause that he'd always been generous when it came to projects like St Luke's stained-glass window fund, the restoration of the gardens around the war memorial and the resurfacing of the children's playground in the park.

In any case, the council had spoken. The deal was done, whether people liked it or not. The complaints had simmered down and Charnley Acre did what it did best, and just got on with it.

Laura sighed. 'I love the Christmas market. It's so festive and it smells marvellous, with the toffee apples and candy and everything. It's an outlet for people to sell their crafts, and the kids love it, too.'

'It hasn't been cancelled,' Clayton said, shaking his head. 'The market's still going ahead. It's being relocated, that's all. Some of the stalls will be in the car park and some along the street itself. That's all been agreed. The council moved fast on that one, for a change.'

'Oh. That's good, then.' Laura realised she didn't sound that pleased about it. Well, shame on her. It was her fault; if she'd stayed in the Ginger Cat for longer she might have had the full story.

So, why had Clayton not told her that in the first place, instead of letting her drag him all the way up here for nothing?

'Not that simple,' Clayton said.

'It sounds it.'

'The council needed to give permission for the stalls to operate from the car park and the street, which they did, as I said. All the stalls except mine. Selling Christmas trees, apparently, is a different thing altogether. Whoever rubber-stamped the gifts and sweets and all that sort of thing refused to issue the necessary for my little enterprise.' Seeing Laura's face, Clayton threw up his hands. 'I know. You tell me. Something about selling trees being purely for profit and not in the same community spirit of entertainment as the rest of the market.'

Laura was appalled. 'That can't be right. Have you appealed?'

'I tried. The council won't budge, and that's that.'

'But what's it to them? It's just another stall. And it's one of the most festive things in the damn market, plus, it's a kind of public service, profit or not. People rely on you for a decent tree, and nowhere else in the village sells them.' This was true. The greengrocers in the high street didn't sell Christmas trees, nor did any other shop. Not everybody wanted to go to a garden centre or a supermarket, miles away. It was *so* unfair.

'It is a bit of a mystery, I know. The reasons I was given sounded pretty vague. I did ask if I could set up somewhere else in the village, separate from the Christmas market, but there's nowhere it wouldn't cause an obstruction. I can see that. So, it seems there's naff all I can do about it. In any case, time's running out. I haven't got time to fight it anymore. My order for the trees has already gone in to the plantation.'

'My offer hasn't come a moment too soon, then?' Laura smiled a question.

'If I'm understanding you right, no, it certainly hasn't. Look, Laura, are you really sure about my setting up shop in your garden?'

There was a wariness in Clayton's tone. There was still a question there about her motivation, then.

'I am, totally. There's that flattish grassed area in front of the rhododendrons which should be big enough. You know the spot I mean. You've mowed it enough times. Customers can park up here, by the house. You could put up a sign by my gate, as big as you like, and advertise it around. People would soon find their way.' Spindlewood, Laura's house, was on the outskirts of the village, situated halfway up Charnley Hill. Those who usually bought their tree from Green and Fragrant, which included most of the residents of Charnley Acre, wouldn't have much further to go than before. 'It's a village tradition, your Christmas tree plot, with the carols playing, and the hot chestnuts. People look forward to it. We can't let it go.'

Clayton's eyes widened just perceptibly. She'd said 'we', aligned herself with him with that small word. But this wasn't a matter of taking sides and she hoped Clayton understood that. It was purely business, as Spencer was so fond of saying.

Clayton looked away, turning his gaze towards the kitchen window where the tangled tendrils of wisteria had caught in the wind and were whipping the glass.

'I must cut that back next time,' he said, clearly prevaricating.

Laura sighed. 'It's all right, Clayton. If it's a bad idea let's forget I ever said anything. I'm sure you'll sort out something much better.'

'No.' Clayton's head snapped round. 'It's a great idea. Thanks, Laura. I'll pay you a fair price for the use of the space, obviously.'

'You accept?'

'Why not? It's a business arrangement. I can work with that.'

Laura frowned. That was an odd thing to say, wasn't it? It was almost as if Clayton was trying to convince himself. Okay, having Spencer and Clayton ostensibly on opposing sides wasn't ideal but as Clayton had said, the fight was over; it was time to move on. He was being cautious because of her involvement with Spencer – she understood that – but it didn't have to be that complicated. And in any case, Christmas would be over in a flash, sadly. Yes, it was all going to be fine. She got up out of her chair.

'Come on, let's walk down and have a proper look at the space.'

If there'd been any doubt in Clayton's mind before, there was no sign of it as they walked down the drive. He strode on eagerly, and Laura had to lengthen her own stride to keep up with him.

'Here, yes?' Clayton smiled at Laura as they reached the spot she had in mind.

'Yes. You can spread out as far as you want to.'

Clayton stood in the middle of the grassy space and spun round in a circle with his arms flung wide, making Laura laugh. They'd passed Saul on the way. He'd looked up from filling the sacks with debris from the flower borders, and now his curiosity brought him down to join them.

'Bloody marvellous,' Saul said, when Clayton had explained.

'Language.' Clayton shot Saul a look and raised his eyes at Laura.

'Sorry.' Saul gazed around as if he was seeing something wonderful instead of a patch of grass. 'Tis though. It's perfect. Thanks, Lau... Mrs Engleby.'

Laura smiled. 'Laura will do.'

Saul probably couldn't believe his luck, now he knew he'd be spending his days on Holly's home ground.

'You're very welcome,' she said. 'I'm glad my garden will be of some use, and not just something pretty to look at.'

Clayton turned to Laura. 'You do realise the grass'll get churned up where people are constantly treading? I'll lay some boards down, which will help protect it but it won't be pristine afterwards.'

'Oh, I'm not worried about that. The grass will recover, won't it? You'll have to give it some of your special TLC afterwards.'

'Yep, TLC is what it will get, in spades. Literally, if necessary.' Clayton smiled at Laura, a kind of private smile that made it hard to look away. He turned to Saul. 'Bring the sacks down and stick them in the van if you're done. We mustn't hold Mrs Engleby up any longer.'

'I'll be in touch about the dates and the deliveries and so on,' he said, addressing Laura.

'Fine. I'll look forward to it.'

Laura went indoors as Clayton started up the van. Resisting the urge to run upstairs to the turret room and watch the van pulling away from Spindlewood, she went to the kitchen and slowly washed up the two mugs in the sink while gazing out at the wintry back garden.

Had she just made a stupid mistake? Only time would tell.

CHAPTER 2

Laura stood the mugs on the draining board, went through to the dining room and looked askance at the colourful pile of graffitied folders laid out on the table. She wasn't in the mood for work now, but she'd set aside the rest of Saturday morning to finish marking this lot. If she put it off now, she'd be doing it at ten o'clock on Sunday night. It wouldn't be the first time.

Laura taught children with special educational needs, at a small, friendly school nestled in a crook of the South Downs, five miles from Charnley Acre. She loved her job; the hard work was satisfying and rewarding but not, unfortunately, in a financial way. This wouldn't have been a problem if Spindlewood wasn't rapidly turning into a money pit. As if to remind her of this, a gust of wind set the dining-room windows rattling. On the sill of the smaller window, a small pool of rainwater had gathered in the night. Laura ignored it, sat down, and opened the top folder. A stream of wonky writing met her, pages of crooked lettering with hardly any breaks between the words, but there'd be a story in there somewhere, with any luck. Pushing the problem of the house and its ever encroaching needs out of her mind, she picked up her pen. Spindlewood had waited long enough. It could wait again, at least until after Christmas.

The windows of the elegant, oak-panelled dining room overlooked the front of the house. Hearing the sound of an approaching vehicle, Laura looked up. Moments later, she was opening the door to her friend, Emily, and Wilf, Emily's ten-year-old black-and-white whippet.

'Saved by the bell.' She gave Emily a kiss on the cheek.

'I didn't get to ring it. Saved from what?'

'Marking.' Laura raised her eyes.

'If you will be a teacher, what d'you expect?' Emily came into the hall, bringing a wave of cold air with her. She went straight through to the kitchen, Wilf trotting behind her. 'Two mugs? Have I interrupted a Saturday morning lovers' tryst?' She pointed meaningfully up at the ceiling.

'I told you, I was marking. And no, Spencer's not here, if that's what you mean,' Laura said. 'If you must know, it was Clayton Masters. He came to see me earlier. We had things to discuss.'

Emily looked surprised. 'Clayton, as in man of the soil? What were you discussing? Garden pest control?'

Laura laughed. 'I'll tell you, if you let me get a word in edgeways.'

She grabbed her navy-blue duffle coat from the hook on the back of the door. Since Clayton's visit she'd felt strangely unsettled, and now she wanted to be outdoors again.

Emily shrugged, caught Wilf by his collar and followed Laura out into the garden. Passing the shrubbery, they went up the short flight of stone steps and headed along the path that led beneath the rose arch. Beyond the arch, the path opened onto a circular paved area with a carved stone bird bath in the centre and a blue-painted iron bench facing it. Laura sat down and

Emily followed suit. The bench felt damp and chilly, like the day itself.

Laura loved the garden in winter, as much as she did the rest of the year. Orange leaves clung stubbornly to black branches, scarlet dogwood lit the shrubbery, and they'd seen several roses still in bloom along the path. The bare twigs and stems of resting plants had a charm of their own, creating stark but beautiful shapes in the borders, as if they'd been sketched in ink by an artistic hand.

Emily wasn't prepared to wait any longer. 'So, come on then. What's afoot with the cute gardener?'

Laura smothered a smile at her friend's description of Clayton but didn't pick up on it; that was one conversation best left alone. She told Emily about the Christmas trees. Again, surprise crossed Emily's face. She did a little double take.

Laura frowned. 'It's not that wild an idea, surely?'

'No, I suppose not. I was only thinking that after the ruckus in the Goose the other night you might have been a bit more circumspect, that's all.'

'What ruckus?'

'Surely you've heard. It's all over the village!'

'Not quite all over if it hasn't reached here.'

Laura was puzzled. She didn't have to stay that way for long. Clearly with some delight, Emily launched into a wildly vivid account of the stand-up row between Spencer and Clayton that had, apparently, happened in the Goose and Feather last Monday night. Emily hadn't been there at the time, she said, but it seemed that those who were had made no secret of what was said, or rather shouted, by both parties. Unsurprisingly, it was all about the development site.

Laura sighed. 'Are they still arguing about that? I thought everyone had got over it.'

'You'd have thought so, wouldn't you?'

Emily's version of events was typically colourful, becoming more so as she warmed to her story. Accusations had flown from both sides, Laura heard; some reasonable, others not, but spewed out in the heat of the argument. Laura took some of this with a large pinch of salt – Emily loved a drama – but the fact that there had been an argument couldn't be disputed.

When Emily had finished her story, Laura sat quietly, trying to take all this in. The rancour between the two men was baffling, as well as acutely sad. Surely Spencer understood why Clayton was so strongly opposed to his scheme? In his line of business as a property developer, he must face opposition all the time. He was used to handling it, and it wasn't personal. What was different about this particular dispute that had caused him to make a spectacle of himself in public? And, as for Clayton, from what Laura knew of him, virtually fighting with Spencer in the pub seemed entirely out of character. Laura felt a rush of shame for Spencer, having acted so unprofessionally. She wasn't too keen on her gardener's involvement, either.

But it did explain Clayton's hesitation over accepting her offer of the use of her garden. He couldn't have known that the pub episode had passed her by.

'I wouldn't worry,' Emily said. 'You know what pub banter's like once it gets going.'

'Hardly banter, if it was anything like you said.'

What was she supposed to do now? It wasn't up to her to do anything, though, was it? If Clayton could ride this out and set up shop in her front garden, knowing her connection to Spencer and that he was likely to show up at the house at any time, then so be it.

The whole situation had blown up out of all proportion; that was the truth of it, Emily asserted now. She put it down to male pride. Put two women in that situation and they'd have agreed to differ and have done with it.

'I do hope you're right,' Laura said.

She had an awful vision of her boyfriend and her gardener battling it out, possibly physically, in the middle of her lawn, with Christmas carols as incidental music. That *would* give the village something to talk about. Laura smiled to herself, and switched her thoughts back to the positive. The Christmas tree sales plot would bring an added air of festivity to Spindlewood and nobody, especially not the two supposedly grown men in question, was going to spoil it.

She got up from the bench. 'It's getting nippy. Let's go in and I'll make coffee, if you've got time.'

'I've *always* got time,' Emily said, pulling a face.

That wasn't quite true. Emily, who described herself as joyfully divorced, was a journalist on the local weekly newspaper, the *Cliffhaven News*, and crammed her time off with endless activity. Her remark was an oblique reference to her forays into the world of internet dating, which had so far been a failure – according to Emily anyway.

'No luck in the love market, I suppose?' said Laura.

'You suppose right. There was one bloke whose profile said he had his own set of power tools. That might've been handy. I could've sent him over here when I'd finished with him.'

They both laughed. Emily called Wilf, and they walked back along the rose path. Laura automatically looked up at the house as they reached the top of the steps. A couple of roof tiles had come loose, just above her bedroom window. Those would have to be seen to before the wind got under them and lifted them off completely. Each new failing the house displayed nailed home the truth that she couldn't afford the upkeep.

Built in 1901 of Edwardian red brick, with tall chimneys straight out of Enid Blyton, and the turret with its gnome-cap roof, the house had been James's dream before it was hers. But it hadn't taken her long to appreciate its airy rooms and fairy-tale charm, at which point she'd fallen in love with the house completely. They'd bought it for a song because of its run-down state, then scrimped and saved, and lived in a couple of rooms with baby Holly until they could afford to make it habitable, doing much of the work themselves.

Even when Holly was growing up and had begun to look at life beyond the backwater of a Sussex village, they had never dreamed of selling. Instead they'd planned how they would spread themselves out and just enjoy living here.

And then, the unthinkable had happened: James had died of cancer, indecently fast, it seemed, once he'd been diagnosed. He'd been almost twenty years older than Laura, but still only sixty when he died. So much of James's income as manager of a haulage company, as well as his inheritance from his parents, had been poured into Spindlewood. They would have made better plans for the future, had there been time, but all that had seemed such a long way off. Yet here she was at forty-five, having already been widowed for five years.

'Every time I look at the house, I can't help thinking it won't be mine for much longer,' she said.

Emily looked at her in dismay. 'Oh, don't say that, Laura. It's so sad. You can't think of selling up. All your memories are here.'

'I can take my memories with me but what I can't do is watch the place falling down around my ears.' Laura laughed to lighten the moment. She didn't want to feel sad. 'I don't expect it will come to that.'

They'd reached the back door. Emily went ahead and made straight for the kettle. Laura stood with her arms folded, gazing out of the window at the wintry garden.

'Maybe I could take in lodgers. I've got two spare bedrooms and an attic with potential.'

'You'd *hate* that, having strangers about the place.'

'I know I would. I could put up with it if I had to, though.

Plenty of people do. In any case, this house is way too big for just one person, two when Holly's home, and she'll be off before long, making her own life, as she should.'

Who was Laura trying to convince? Emily, or herself? The thing about the house being too big for one person had come from a throwaway remark of Spencer's. He hadn't actually said she should think about downsizing, but the implication had been there. He was good at that, dropping an idea into her head while pretending he wasn't serious. She'd taken no notice at the time, but clearly his words had struck a chord, somewhere deep inside her brain.

She turned to Emily. 'I really don't want to sell Spindlewood.'

'Then, of course you mustn't. Anyway, if you moved into some pokey cottage, where would you put your mum and your sister and her lot when they come and stay, like at Christmas, for instance?' Emily grinned. 'You know the answer, don't you? Marry Spencer, or at least let him move in. He'd soon sort the house out.'

It wasn't the first time Emily had suggested that, and only half in jest.

Laura giggled. 'He'd sort it out all right. He'd probably want to flatten the whole thing and build a block of flats.' Emily raised an eyebrow. 'Don't worry, I'm only joking.'

But already, Laura's thoughts had veered away from the problems of the house. She and Spencer were going out to dinner tonight, to the Ashley Arms, in a nearby village. Should she tell him about Clayton's Christmas trees being sold at Spindlewood, or would that be adding fuel to a fire that might be about to burn out of its own accord? He'd have to know some time, though, and there was no rational reason why he should make an issue of it. As usual, she was probably worrying for nothing.

CHAPTER 3

'You've told him *what*?' Spencer looked up suddenly from his seafood risotto as if he couldn't believe what he'd heard.

'I've told Clayton Masters he can sell his Christmas trees from the garden at Spindlewood. He needs somewhere, I have somewhere. It makes perfect sense.'

Spencer speared a prawn, somewhat savagely. 'To you, maybe. Well, I hope you know what you're doing, Laura, that's all. You're setting a precedent. What happens next year, and the one after?'

'I'll worry about that when the time comes,' Laura said, her inner voice whispering that the time might not come at all. 'If you'd have let Clayton stay where he was for one more Christmas, he wouldn't have had to find somewhere in such a hurry.'

Spencer shook his head. 'That was never an option. I'm putting surveyors on the job in a week or so. Your tree man would be in the way.'

'He's not *my* tree man...'

Laura sighed. She didn't want to argue, especially when she

had no chance of winning. That ship had already sailed. She smiled in an attempt to lighten the moment.

'Let's not talk about it anymore. Here, try this pork. It's delicious.' She held out her fork with a piece of sage-infused tenderloin on it.

Spencer took the morsel into his mouth. 'Great.' Then, after a moment, he said, 'I don't like the idea of your private property being invaded by strangers.'

So much for dropping the subject.

'Hardly *invaded*. They won't all be strangers either. Most of the customers will come from the village.'

Spencer held up his hands. 'I'm only looking out for you, Laura, that's all.'

'Nothing to do with your feud with Clayton, then?'

The words were out before she could stop them. She'd intended to keep the conversation general, but Spencer was showing a touch of arrogance, which was unusual for him and she didn't like it.

Spencer looked surprised, then faintly alarmed. Clearly he hadn't intended to tell Laura himself about the to-do in the Goose and Feather, but he should have known she'd find out eventually.

'Not at all,' Spencer said emphatically – too emphatically to Laura's mind. 'It's *not* a feud, only a slight disagreement between businessmen, that's all. It's not personal.'

Not personal? Then why the display in front of half the village?

Laura stayed silent. She sipped her half-glass of red wine; she'd brought her own car tonight. For some reason, she hadn't wanted Spencer to pick her up, as he usually did. Sometimes, she felt like sitting back and enjoying letting him look after her, and at others, like tonight, her independent nature clamoured to be asserted.

'Not that Clayton of Green and Fragrant, or whatever it's called, *is* a proper businessman, in the real sense of the word,' added Spencer, in an offhand voice which said more than his actual words.

Laura saw red. 'What do you mean by that? Clayton runs a highly successful business, he provides a great service and lots of people rely on him, like I do. Just because he gets his hands dirty there's no need to be snobby about it.'

'I'm *not* being snobby...'

Spencer glanced towards a nearby party of four who were undisguisedly showing interest, and shot Laura a warning look, but she didn't care who was listening. She'd had enough. Just because Spencer had made a mint out of property development, it didn't give him the right to knock a small business like Clayton's. The two enterprises weren't comparable for a start, and she happened to know that Spencer's company had begun with a substantial injection of cash from his father; she doubted Clayton had been so fortunate.

She threw down her napkin and pushed back her chair.

'Laura...?' Spencer stood up too, reaching a placating hand across the table, his eyes full of alarm, and concern. 'Sit down, finish your meal. We'll talk about something else, I promise.'

Laura hesitated, then she said, 'I'm sorry, Spencer, it's not just that. I've got a splitting headache and I'm really not hungry anymore.' Picking up her bag, she crossed the bar full of diners and headed for the door.

It wasn't only Spencer's attitude towards Clayton that had spiked her need to be away from him; she realised that as soon as she was standing beneath the fairy lights in the porch, breathing deeply. It was more than that, but her mind refused to focus on what else it might be. She took more deep breaths, inhaling the sharp air with its hint of frost. Her car was only yards away; she could be in it and away in seconds, but she couldn't do that to Spencer. Being out here alone was doing a fair job in calming her down.

A pair of tall, fake Christmas trees stood one each side of the entrance to the pub garden. They always decorated early here; it pulled the customers in. The trees were frosty white, strewn with hundreds of tiny white lights which twinkled like stars. From the branches hung oversized, clear glass baubles on silver ribbon, silver bells on red ribbon, and white sparkly snowmen wearing red and green scarves. Laura gazed at the trees and felt better. She loved Christmas and all the trappings that went with it. She couldn't wait to fetch her own tree down from the attic, and all the decorations that came out faithfully, year after year.

But shouldn't she have a real tree this year, one purchased from Green and Fragrant? They'd always had a real tree in James's time. It was only in recent years she'd taken the easier option, but perhaps this year she should return to tradition. Holly would like that. She imagined herself looking over Clayton's trees for just the right one. Clayton, helpful as he was, would carry it up to the house for her. He might even offer to help her put it in place. But if she said no, she could manage, he wouldn't insist. Spencer, on the other hand, would assume that putting up a Christmas tree was most definitely a man's job, and all she was capable of was hanging the baubles.

Goodness, where were these thoughts coming from? Why was her mind set on drawing comparisons between her gardener and the man whom she might, possibly, spend the rest of her life with? It was too bad of her, it really was. She felt slightly guilty but relieved when she felt a hand on her shoulder. She turned around, leaning in to curve herself against the solid warmth of Spencer's chest.

'I'm sorry, Spence. I felt a bit off for a moment but I'm all right now.' She peeled away from him and smiled. 'Do you want to go back inside and have a dessert, or coffee?'

'No, I'm good. Let's call it a night, shall we? We don't want your headache getting worse.' His eyes gleamed in the soft light of the porch, the fairy lights above casting miniature pools of colour on his dark hair.

'You've got a rainbow in your hair,' Laura said, reaching up to touch the crown of his head.

Spencer raised his hand and caught hold of hers, taking it to his lips to press a kiss on her fingers. 'I'm so sorry if I upset you. I never meant to. I do love you, Laura.'

'Yes, I know.'

They walked across the gravelled forecourt to where the cars were parked, Spencer's arm loosely around Laura's shoulders.

'Ah, two cars,' Spencer said, as if he'd forgotten they'd arrived separately. 'What's it to be? Shall I follow you home, then? Unless you want to follow me?'

Laura felt unaccountably irritated. It wasn't as though Spencer expected every date to end with sex, either at hers or his, although it often did. She wasn't being fair on him, in her mind. But tonight her mind seemed to have a different agenda. If only she could work out what it was.

'Do you mind if it's not either?' She smiled, placing a hand on Spencer's chest. 'Come to lunch tomorrow, if you like.'

It felt as if she was offering him a consolation prize. His face showed he was thinking the same. Really, she was too tired for this, too tired to negotiate, or to worry that she'd hurt Spencer's feelings.

'Of course I don't mind. You get home and have a good night's sleep. I'll be busy tomorrow but I'll ring you.'

Once she was home, Laura couldn't bring herself to go straight to bed, tired though she was. Her dinner date with Spencer hadn't been easy, and therefore it hadn't been much fun either. It was her fault – well, partly. The moment she'd seen the way it was heading, she should have nipped the conversation about Clayton in the bud right away and smoothed it over. Instead, she'd come out of her corner fighting and made it a whole lot worse.

But that was just it. She still wasn't sure what it had all been about, not really. If there was more to all this than appeared on the surface, Spencer wasn't saying, and she certainly wouldn't learn anything from Clayton.

Laura went through to the kitchen. She made herself some tea and took a couple of paracetamol – it was true, she did have a niggling headache – then went upstairs to the turret room. Without turning on the light, she stood by the uncurtained window, cradling her mug of tea. There was no moon tonight – it was lost in the murky winter sky – but there was just enough light to show the stark outlines of the trees, black against charcoal.

Spindlewood stood on a rise. At the front of the house, the grounds sloped gently downwards to the road, levelling out halfway down, at the spot Laura had earmarked for the Christmas tree plot. She stared through the gloom, sensing rather than seeing the undulating lawns which wrapped around the house, and the deep herbaceous borders, so wonderfully colourful in season. If she did have to leave here, she would miss the garden as much as the house.

Thinking about the garden brought Clayton back to mind; not that he'd been far from it. It was all very well blaming Spencer for overreacting to her news, but had she not done the same thing, rushing out of the pub like a stroppy teenager? It must have been as perplexing to Spencer as it was to her. Well, she'd make it up to him. She would invite him to dinner tomorrow instead of lunch and let him stay over, even though it was a school night. And she would try, if possible, to keep well away from the subject of Christmas trees, and Clayton.

The grandmother clock chimed twelve. Laura shivered in the slight draught. Taking a last look out of the window, she visualised the miniature, transitory pine forest that was about to appear in her garden, and smiled into the darkness.

CHAPTER 4

Spencer pulled the BMW off the Charnley road into a mud-rutted layby, switched off the engine and leaned back in his seat. Through the glass, the winter sun was warm on his face. For two pins, he could drop off to sleep, right now; it was only 2pm. It had been a stressful week in which nothing had gone right. Well, nothing had gone his way, which amounted to the same thing.

He'd just come from the Uckfield site where he'd discovered a problem, or rather, the builders working on it had. A row of three tiny terraced cottages, uninhabited, had been demolished, which had drawn minimal opposition from the locals since they were riddled with damp, woodworm and goodness knows what else. If he hadn't demolished them, they'd have fallen down of their own accord. He planned to put up two decent-sized houses in their place, lovely modern interiors but the exteriors done in what was called sympathetic style, to fit with the surrounding Victorian buildings. That wasn't the problem. No, the problem was that dreadful stuff called Japanese knotweed.

The construction manager, a doom merchant if ever there was one, had presented him with the evidence of the pernicious weed with something amounting to glee. He'd waved the fragments of its roots in front of Spencer for his inspection as soon as he'd arrived on site. The bloke was some kind of expert on the subject, or so he made out, and Spencer had no reason to dispute it. Japanese knotweed, he'd blithely informed Spencer, as if he didn't already have a rough idea how insidious the stuff was, could grow up to ten centimetres a day and its stems could reach up to four metres in height. It had been cut back and possibly treated with chemicals in the past, but that hadn't done the job properly. The stuff still lurked beneath the back gardens of the old cottages, creeping none too shyly into what remained of the walls and foundations.

Okay, the problem wasn't insurmountable – was anything, when push came to shove? Although it wasn't illegal to have Japanese knotweed on your property, it was against the law to allow it to spread elsewhere. In other words, Spencer being the current owner of the site, it was solely his responsibility to get rid of it before the surveyors got word of it, which no doubt they would. That kind of secret never stayed secret, and Spencer was damned if he was going to end up being prosecuted over a plant.

There were experts in the field, experts that would have to be called in, firstly to clear the site of knotweed, and secondly, most importantly, to advise properly on the legal obligations – Spencer's obligations – and to act on his behalf if necessary. All that would cost time and money, a lot of money, and cause the job to overrun. He couldn't afford for that to happen. But what choice did he have? He'd left the site with a firm instruction to the builders to get on with the job and leave him to deal with the rest. God knew when he'd have time to do that, but he'd have to make time, that was clear. For once, this wasn't an issue that could be solved with a return favour or a backhander.

Spencer's other problem, or possibly problems plural – he wasn't sure yet – were two-fold. His professional and personal reputation were suddenly, alarmingly, at stake, in ways he'd never envisaged, as well as his relationship with Laura Engleby. True, it had been a risk returning to Charnley Acre after he'd gone home to Gloucestershire to escape any fallout from that dreadful business. But that was five years ago. He should be free to live where it suited him and, for now, Charnley Acre suited him very well. He'd always liked the area. He had connections in this part of Sussex, and there were opportunities to grow his business. Gloucestershire had been the centre of his world for the first twenty years of his life, apart from one or two sojourns elsewhere, and he'd had enough of it. Visiting his family was all well and good; he just didn't need to base himself within spitting distance.

Bedsides, it wasn't as if he was guilty of anything, as the court had ruled, but everyone knew that mud, if thrown accurately, tended to stick. With this in mind, and his business reputation to protect, he'd taken certain precautions, which should have been enough.

Until he'd run right into Clayton Masters, at Laura's house, of all places.

Stupidly, he'd never thought to look up the man and see if he was still in the area. In his mind, Clayton was a feature of the past, a very unpleasant feature. Considering what had happened to him, he would surely have moved on somewhere else. Having ruled this as a high probability early on, Spencer had given the man no further thought.

The shock at the chance meeting had affected them both, that had been apparent at the time. But Spencer had rapidly regrouped, made it perfectly plain by his body language that he and Laura were together, and brazened it out. It wasn't as if Masters was Laura's guest, nor even her friend, although they had seemed at ease with each other. He was just the gardener, the hired help. He was nobody.

And then the whole thing had become a hundred times worse when Spencer discovered that he and Clayton were inextricably linked by his proposed new housing development. Spencer couldn't believe it when he'd heard about the Christmas tree sales being part of the village's Christmas market. He'd had the pleasure of finding that out at the first open meeting where, along with a couple of colleagues, he'd been prepared to field any awkward questions and reassure the locals that his company's development was in the public interest. But so, apparently, was the market, and the damn Christmas tree enterprise. Clayton had wasted no time in making that point, staunchly backed by a number of other attendees who'd joined in quite volubly.

Only Spencer and Masters himself had known the fight was personal, as well as about business and the village community. Intensely personal.

So, his big concern now was whether Clayton had told Laura about their miserable shared history. If he had, Laura hadn't mentioned it. Which meant either that the gardener hadn't spilled his guts to his employer, or he had, and Laura had decided to keep quiet about it. For now.

Honestly, if there were two people who should be kept apart from one another, it was Laura Engleby and Clayton Masters. Spencer sighed as he considered, for the millionth time, the effect on him if Laura got to hear Clayton's take on the story. It would be a pack of lies, but who was to say she wouldn't believe him? And if she did, how bloody awful it would be, as well as inconvenient, if Spencer then had to go to the trouble of defending himself and talking Laura round? Just when he was getting somewhere with her, too.

She couldn't find out, that was the bottom line. She just couldn't. But quite how Spencer was going to prevent it from happening he had no idea.

The sun streaming through the window had suddenly got unbearably hot. He opened the door and stepped out. He felt claustrophobic and slightly nauseous. Treading either side of the muddy ruts in his polished shoes, he went and stood at the gate that opened onto a ploughed field. The shock of the cold compared with the inside of the car made him hike in his breath sharply but he felt better for it. Turning up the collar of his coat, he leaned on the top bar of the gate.

Laura was an amazing woman, one of the best, if not *the* best, he'd ever been out with. She was definitely the first he'd thought he could handle a permanent relationship with, and that was saying something. He'd been instantly drawn to her, realised she was someone special. And then, he'd seen Spindlewood, and the cogs in his brain had sped up, making the prospect of being with Laura even more bright and shiny.

He shouldn't have caused that scene in the Ashley Arms the other night. Spencer didn't regret much in his life but he definitely regretted that. It had been a shock, and a pretty nasty one at that, finding out that Clayton Masters would be setting up shop in Laura's garden in order to flog his no doubt overpriced Christmas trees to an unsuspecting public. Why was she doing it? It made no sense whatsoever. Okay, so Spencer's little plan of robbing Clayton of a tidy sum had failed. A word in the right ear and he'd succeeded in blocking the council's permission for the tree site to move alongside the other displaced Christmas market stalls – an expensive but necessary action. But it was more than that. The little arrangement between Laura and her gardener indicated a certain closeness, a kind of friendship, which could only deepen, the more time the pair of them spent together. And friends shared secrets, didn't they? Confided in one another. It would only take a few of the right words in the wrong direction and Spencer's cover would be blown sky high.

All this had run swiftly through his mind as Laura had made

her announcement. And then, stupidly, he'd gone right ahead and challenged her so strongly she must have wondered what he'd got against the tree idea, and, even more, what he'd got against the seller of the trees.

He'd been surprised at first when he realised she knew all about the altercation in the Goose, but he shouldn't have been. In a village like Charnley Acre, word of that kind of thing soon got about. That was something else he regretted, goading Clayton in public. He'd only gone in for a quiet pint, but the barman knew who he was, and naturally they'd chatted about the housing development. It had been innocuous chat, the barman being more interested in the style of houses he'd be putting up and whether they'd really be within the means of young families on lowish incomes. That was the plan, Spencer had assured him, hopefully boosting up his altruistic credentials.

Then, Spencer had spotted Clayton, and the man had clearly had an ear to his private conversation with the barman.

It had all kicked off from there. Spencer wasn't entirely blameless, he'd be the first to admit it. Six of one, half a dozen of the other. But it had escalated, as these things did, and now Laura seemed to be blaming him. In fact, she'd nailed her colours to the mast, coming right out and defending Clayton as she had. No wonder he'd seen red. Spencer wasn't an unreasonable man, not at all. He just wanted to make the best of an unfortunate situation. But Laura couldn't seem to grasp that. She'd rushed out of the Ashley in a strop, leaving Spencer sitting alone at the table looking like a total loser.

They'd made it up, of course. But the whole episode had left Spencer with a sour taste in his mouth as his worries increased, and he'd not even had the consolation of going to bed with her at the end of the night.

Spencer peeled himself away from the gate and got back in

the car. He couldn't leave things as they were. It was too chancy. He had feelings for Laura, feelings he expressed often in the accepted manner. She was gorgeous, sexy and he enjoyed her company. She was also the owner of a big old house that was ripe for development. Nothing could be allowed to get in the way of either cause.

He would have to tell her straight. Well, straight*ish*. Appeal to her better judgement and her sense of loyalty to him; play on her emotions. He was her partner, after all, and she should put him first. All he had to do was find the right words, a skill that seemed to have deserted him recently. He would be fair but firm when he told Laura she was to have nothing more to do with Clayton Masters.

That decided, Spencer started the car and pulled out onto the road. He had intended to drive straight home but maybe it wouldn't hurt to make a little detour to Spindlewood and check how the land lay, as it were.

CHAPTER 5

Clayton strode along the back garden path of his home, Mistletoe Cottage, and unlocked the double doors of the corrugated-roofed shed. Scouting around, he found what he needed – two pairs of extra-long tree-loppers – and lifted them out. As he locked the doors and headed back to the van, he sent up a silent prayer of thanks for the Sunday morning telly gardening programme which helped sustain people's interest in their plots at this time of the year. Not that he would necessarily have chosen late November to cull the branches of the particular trees the owner had in mind, but he had to make a living, and mostly he was happy to follow the wishes of the customers, unless there was any danger of serious damage. Despite the prompt of the latest celebrity gardener, business naturally slackened off in winter, which was where the Christmas tree sales came in, providing a much needed boost to his income.

Throwing the loppers into the back of the van, he nipped back indoors to collect his personal belongings before climbing into the driver's seat. As he started up and pulled out into Squirrel Lane, Clayton sent up a second prayer, this time thanking Laura Engleby for coming to his rescue over the Christmas trees.

When she'd first approached him with her suggestion, through the window of the van when they were parked in the high street, she'd seemed unsure of herself, even a little embarrassed, which wasn't like Laura at all from what he knew of her. In fact, he'd go so far as to say she'd wished she could have retracted her words.

He'd understood her perfectly well, of course; she'd invited him to sell the trees from her garden, simple as that. But, because of her uncertain manner at the time, it had felt wrong to seal the deal there and then, which was why he'd agreed to her suggestion to go up to Spindlewood and discuss it properly. Not the only reason, if he was honest, but he didn't want to think about that. Instead, he thought about Marcus Dartnell – or Spencer Jennings, as he called himself now.

Clayton had been downright shocked when, on his third only visit to Spindlewood, he'd come face to face with Marcus. He'd known for a fact that the man had left Charnley Acre years before, right after it happened, and scuttled back to the family home in Gloucestershire. Clayton had never expected, nor wanted, to set eyes on him ever again.

It had been a warm, sunny morning. Mrs Engleby – Laura – had come along the path where he and Saul had been putting up a new trellis for the climbing roses and asked if they'd like to come in for some tea, but they were busy that day, with several more bookings ahead of them. He'd had a flask with him anyway, and Saul had a ready supply of Cokes in the van.

And then, just as Laura had turned to go back to the house, the unmistakable figure of Marcus Dartnell had shadowed the space at the end of the path. His eyes had met Clayton's with equal shock. When Laura had casually introduced him as Spencer, Clayton's stare had hardened even more as they'd exchanged the obligatory nod. Then Marcus had put a proprietorial arm around Laura's waist and, with a final loaded glance at Clayton, had drawn her away.

Marcus Dartnell. Clayton's sworn enemy. And he didn't have many of those. No others at all, in fact. Clayton wasn't given to hating, or even disliking, anyone. In his book, there was always a reason for the way people behaved, if you only knew. But for Marcus he made an exception. No reasons, no excuses, just...

A black cat shot across Squirrel Lane, causing Clayton to brake and bringing his mind sharply back to the present. He steered the van out onto the main road before he let his thoughts wander again, this time towards Laura Engleby. How could a woman as lovely as her be in a relationship with someone like Marcus? It had been all Clayton could do not to challenge her about it; make sure she knew what kind of man she'd got herself involved with. Did she even know he wasn't using his real name? He'd bet his life she had no idea. But it was just a fantasy conversation, pointlessly rehearsed inside his head. It could never happen in reality. He was the gardener; his employer's private life was none of his business. What was more, he'd had to train his mind to think of the man as Spencer, not Marcus, in case he inadvertently blurted it out in front of Laura.

Much as Clayton had tried to justify Spencer's presence at Spindlewood, it was obvious what his status was; he'd passed the man driving out of Laura's gate at eight in the morning. What was almost as galling was that, leaving aside the kerfuffle over the development site which already showed signs of blowing over, most of the locals thought Spencer Jennings was one of the best. It was easy to be taken in by a well-dressed, well-spoken man who strode around the village, exuding bonhomie at every corner, and forking out a bundle for the latest good cause. So, he had a ready smile and money to burn. Didn't make him a better bloke, did it? It didn't make amends for what he'd done.

Nothing could do that.

Clayton had almost spilled the beans in the Goose and Feather the other night, once he'd got into his stride. He hadn't, of course, because of Laura, and how hurt and humiliated she'd be if she found out in that way.

Since that first confrontation in Laura's garden, Clayton had managed a gruff greeting if he ran into Spencer when Laura was present, and Spencer had done likewise. Otherwise, by silent mutual agreement, the two men ignored each other. But that had changed when the plans for the housing development were made public. Clayton had attended the meeting in the village hall, and there he had exchanged more words with Spencer than he had since the bloke had turned up in Charnley Acre like the proverbial bad penny.

As for the unfortunate scene in the Goose, that had been entirely down to Spencer. Clayton had been minding his own business, enjoying a quiet pint and a game of darts with a couple of mates, and Spencer, sitting up at the bar, had been going on about his 'victory' with the planners, like he was some sort of local hero. His voice had been raised, making sure Clayton heard. What was he to do but stand up and tell Spencer exactly what he thought? As if he didn't know already. But that wasn't the point. Clayton wasn't going to sit there and keep schtum, as if he was some kind of namby-pamby walkover.

The familiar burst of frustration at the arrogance of the man, coupled with a set of brand-new feelings which heightened Clayton's instinctive need to protect Laura, sent his temperature rocketing. His foot reached the brake pedal, pressing unnecessarily hard.

'Hey,' said Saul, getting up from the bus stop bench where

he'd been waiting and levering his long body into the passenger seat. 'What's with the emergency stop?'

Clayton said nothing. Instead, he took a few long breaths to calm himself. Shrugging, Saul plugged himself into his iPod and settled in for the ride to the tree-lopping job.

Four o'clock, and the day was already closing in around him. Having dropped Saul off, Clayton steered the van along the familiar web of narrow roads. The muted browns and greens of the wintry landscape stretched out on either side. Above the South Downs in the distance, the sky had already descended into grey, streaked faintly with pink. It would be December soon; his worst time of the year. The run-up to Christmas was almost harder to bear than the festival itself. Once Christmas arrived, it wasn't too long before he was safely on the other side of it.

Until the next time. Five years, and it never got any better. Would it, ever?

The fork in the road was ahead. Taking a left turn would lead him straight to the village, and home. To the right was Charnley Hill. Without thinking too much about it, Clayton took the right-hand fork. The road climbed gently at first, then more steeply. The van seemed to have a mind of its own as it turned in between the gates of Spindlewood. She might not be in, of course. She was; her car was parked at the top of the drive, in front of the house. Light glowed in one of the downstairs windows. He had an excuse to be here; he wanted to confirm the date the Christmas trees would arrive, and iron out a few details. And they hadn't fixed a day for the wisteria to be cut back. Laura had agreed it needed doing, and there was other trimming and general tidying to be done before winter set in properly. He could have made these arrangements on the phone, of course. But he had been passing, so...

Damn it all, he was here now. There was no need for him to make such a meal of it, was there?

She came to the door before his finger was off the bell. He hoped that didn't indicate that she was annoyed at being disturbed, but he forgot about that as she gave him a warm, welcoming smile.

'I saw the van. Come in. The kettle's on.' She held the door wide to let him in. 'You only just caught me. I've not been home long. I got away early today. Usually it's way after four.'

Clayton remembered her telling him she was a teacher, of special kids at that. He'd bet she was a damn good one. Instead of leading him to the kitchen, she ushered him into the living room where two lamps with blue-and-white ceramic bases the size of oil-drums emitted honeyed pools of light.

'Have a pew,' Laura said cheerfully, waving vaguely towards a couple of huge, plum-coloured sofas. 'I'll bring the tea in.'

Off she went, leaving Clayton to choose his seat. The sofa he sat on had a battered cardboard box perched on the end. Other boxes stood on the floor. Leaning sideways, he peeked into the box on the sofa. Christmas decorations. That was all he needed. Turning his gaze from the other boxes, he distracted himself by looking at the painting on the wall above the fireplace with its ornate tile surround. He'd been in here once before, he remembered, when Laura had invited him through while she fetched his money. He'd admired the fireplace then, but hadn't had time to take in much else. The painting was a landscape of Cuckmere Haven, done in oils.

Laura was back, and saw him looking. 'Beautiful, isn't it? It's by a local artist. James and I used to enjoy walking there.'

'James... your husband?' Clayton knew her husband had died some while back but hadn't known his name.

'Yes. Was.' Laura smiled brightly, giving the impression this wasn't a time for sympathy.

At least she hadn't said she went walking there with Spencer. Clayton felt unduly pleased about that.

Laura handed Clayton his mug of tea then sat down on the floor beside the boxes. She stood her own mug down on the faded carpet. Not only faded but threadbare in a number of places, as were parts of the sofas visible beneath tumbling heaps of multicoloured cushions. The room had a faded elegance about it, coupled with a homely, lived-in feel, the same as the big old kitchen.

'I know it's still only November but I had a sudden urge to sort through the decorations,' Laura said, tugging a tatty string of gold tinsel from one of the boxes and frowning at it. 'Some of this will definitely have to go.'

The whole lot could go as far as Clayton was concerned. He felt the downward tug of depression; he was powerless to stop it. Astute woman that she was, Laura noticed – he could tell by the sudden concern in those blue-grey eyes. He wished her knowingness extended as far as Spencer Jennings.

'I've only just lit the fire,' she said, glancing at the tentative, flickering flames. 'I expect it's like an icebox in here, only I don't notice it myself.'

Rallying, Clayton smiled. 'It's fine. My place is a lot easier to keep snug because it's so small. Could probably fit the whole thing in this room. But there's only me.'

The faint sensation of a blush showed on Laura's cheeks. He hadn't meant to embarrass her but somehow he must have done. Or perhaps it was the heat from the fire that was starting to stoke up nicely.

She laughed, a little awkwardly. 'There's only me here most of the time, and look at the space I've got!'

'It's a beautiful house. Quite a gem.'

'It is, isn't it? I'm so glad you said that.'

Laura turned her attention back to her box of decorations, kneeling up to yank out another tangle of tinsel, and other stuff at random. Clayton didn't look too closely. Instead he looked at Laura herself. She was wearing narrow jeans, with a soft, pale-blue roll-neck jumper and red woollen socks patterned with cartoon sheep. Her shoulder-length straight blonde hair was tucked carelessly behind her ears. As she twisted round, her hair sparkled in the firelight. She moved again, and some of the sparkle loosened itself and fell onto the carpet.

'Look at that. One of the boxes nearly came down on my head when I got it down from the attic. That's very old sparkle, that is.' Laura licked her finger and dabbed up some of the silver fragments. 'Nothing but dust really. I really need to chuck some of this.'

Clayton was silent. He hadn't come here to talk about Christmas decorations, nor to see them unpacked before his eyes. On the other hand, Christmas had to be mentioned since it was the main reason for him turning up without warning. He drew Laura into the subject of dates for the tree sales and other details, and in minutes the thing was sorted, leaving Laura to her festive deliberations.

'Oh, while I remember,' she said, suddenly looking up. She was holding a felt reindeer with bent antlers and a squint. 'I'm having a party on Christmas Eve. Would you like to come? There are some invitations but I haven't got round to giving them out yet. They're only bits of paper, anyway.'

The Christmas Eve parties at Spindlewood were legendary. She hadn't invited him in previous years but he supposed the Christmas tree thing had prompted it. He bit his lip, for the moment stuck for a response.

'Not just you, of course,' Laura said, mistaking his hesitation. 'Bring somebody if you like. Partner, girlfriend, whoever...'

Now, it seemed, it was her turn to lose the power of speech. Kneeling over the box of decorations, she began fumbling about inside. Her hair escaped from behind her ear on one side and fell to hide her face; he sensed she was glad of it.

'Nope. There's nobody like that.' Clayton hoped he sounded non-committal and that she wouldn't take his reply as an acceptance to the invitation. He had no intention of going anywhere near her party.

'Okay. Just you then.' She smiled, and sat back on her heels. 'You'll know a lot of people anyway. Most of them will be the usual suspects from the village.'

Including Spencer, Clayton thought, grimly. Another reason for staying well away. Laura seemed to be waiting for an answer.

'Thanks. I'm not sure what I'm doing yet,' he said.

'Yes, of course. It's early yet, as I said.'

Clayton knew exactly what he'd be doing at Christmas. Shutting the door of Mistletoe Cottage – unfortunate name – and staying put until it was all over. Avoiding Christmas, if such a thing were possible, had become second nature. Selling the trees was okay, though; he could manage that without too much trouble. All he needed to do was exude a bit of false Christmas cheer and think about the money he was making. Get himself into the right mindset, and all would be well.

But he couldn't stop anxiety prickling him, like the damn pine needles, when Laura said, 'I'll put my name on one of your trees, though, if I may. The real ones smell gorgeous once you bring them indoors, don't they?'

Clayton nodded; it was all he could manage. The scent of the tree at Mistletoe Cottage that year had suddenly become unbearable. He'd thrown it out into the garden; lights, decorations and all. One of the first things he'd done after the police had left.

Laura offered him another cup of tea. It was tempting to stay in her company for a while longer, in spite of her decoration-sorting, but she was probably just being polite; it wouldn't do to outstay his welcome. Soon she was seeing him to the door, having arranged a day for him to give the garden what she called its winter tidy.

As the van rattled down the drive, Clayton saw Spencer's dark-blue BMW arriving at the gates. It purred to a standstill on the road outside, waiting for the van to come out before entering. The manoeuvre was completed without either man acknowledging the other.

CHAPTER 6

Laura had only just returned to the living room when she heard the toot of a car horn, and then the chime of the doorbell. Opening the door to Spencer, it took a second for her mind to rearrange itself; her thoughts had still been with Clayton.

'Hello you,' said Spencer, stepping into the hall and gathering her up for a long kiss. 'Mm.' He broke away, gazing intensely into her eyes. 'That was nice.'

His hands roved her body as his mouth searched again for hers. This time she gently turned her head away, putting some space between them.

'I wasn't expecting you.'

'I didn't know I needed to announce myself,' Spencer said, following her through to the living room.

He was clearly trying to sound jokey but it didn't work. Laura turned and glanced curiously at him. Perhaps he'd had a difficult day; she shouldn't be too hard on him.

'I didn't mean that the way it sounded. It's a lovely surprise.'

Laura resumed her place on the floor, with the boxes. 'I was sorting out some of this Christmas stuff but it can wait.'

Spencer sat down in the seat recently vacated by Clayton. He nodded towards the small table between the two sofas.

'Tea for two, was it? I saw the gardener's van.'

Laura felt her shoulders tighten as a sense of déjà vu crept over her. For goodness' sake, was she not allowed to give her gardener a cup of tea without facing the Spanish Inquisition, first from Emily and now Spencer? If her daily life was that fascinating, perhaps she should install a webcam so that nobody missed any detail of it.

'Yes, that's right. Clayton was here. We had arrangements to make.'

She may as well have added, 'What of it?' – it was there, in her tone, as plain as could be.

'Hey.' Spencer held up his hands, the palms facing her. 'I was only passing comment, that's all.'

'I know.' Laura got up from the floor, took the box off the sofa and sat down. 'I'm sorry I snapped. I'm tired, that's all. It's lovely to see you.'

Linking her arms around Spencer's neck, she pulled him to her and planted two light, playful kisses on his mouth. His arms went around her as he kissed her back, not so lightly. After a moment, Laura broke away before the kissing turned into more. Spencer leaned back and crossed his arms, resting his head against the back of the sofa. He looked vaguely disappointed.

Laura suppressed a sigh. She'd been doing this a lot lately, holding back on Spencer, putting up an invisible barrier between them. She didn't mean to do it, but lately she'd begun to wonder exactly how important she was to him. He said he loved her, and she believed him, so why, in that case, had she never met his parents? It wasn't as if he talked about them much either. In fact, they rarely got a mention unless she asked a direct question.

Spencer came from a small town in Gloucestershire, which

was where his parents still lived. He'd told her they were 'getting on a bit' and not in the best of health. His father in particular was quite frail, apparently. She could see how hard it would be for them to come up to Sussex, but surely Spencer could take her to see them, even for a flying visit? They could put up in a hotel or something. He had an elder brother, too, also living in Gloucestershire with a family of his own. From the little information Laura had gleaned through judicious questioning, they sounded nice. She was sure she'd like them all, given the chance. Spencer had met her mother several times, as well as Laura's sister, Rachael – they'd lost Dad three years ago – and they'd all got on well, so why was Spencer dragging his heels over the return match?

Occasionally, Laura carefully raised the subject but all she received each time was a promise that he'd sort something out 'one day'. But that day had never come and she'd begun to think it never would.

She sighed again, this time without hiding it, and Spencer placed his hand over hers and squeezed it gently. Outside, the sky darkened to dusky grey. The fire crackled in the grate.

'You never said why you came, Spence. Not that you need a reason,' Laura said.

'I was passing on my way home from the Uckfield site so I thought I'd pop in. But actually, do you fancy coming over to mine this evening? I'll cook.'

'Oh, that would have been lovely but I've got the book group coming at seven.'

With Clayton's unscheduled visit, and now Spencer's, the book group had gone right out of Laura's mind, until now.

'Ah yes, the book group.' Spencer playfully, and a little annoyingly, flicked the tip of Laura's nose with his finger. 'Not a late one, is it? You could come over to me afterwards, if you like?'

Laura wasn't sure. It was turning out to be a long enough day as it was – an unsettling day, if she was honest.

'I shan't say for definite now but I'll ring you later. Would that be okay?'

'Of course, my lovely, if that's what you want.' He smiled.

Shortly afterwards, Spencer left. He waved cheerily as he spun the BMW round and set off down the drive, flinging up gravel from the back wheels.

On Saturday morning, Laura walked down to the village. She often walked rather than drove; it was such a pretty walk, past a tangle of woods and a stream which bubbled out of the chalk hills, and it was only fifteen minutes to the high street. It was a bright, still day, mild enough not to need a coat over her thick sweater. Spencer was coming over tonight. She'd pick up a couple of fillet steaks at the butchers, which was one of the purposes of the trip. Her other reasons were connected with Christmas.

The preparations were as much fun as Christmas itself; Laura had always thought so, even as a child. When other children, her sister Rachael included, couldn't wait for the big day, Laura had lived in the moment, immersing herself in gluing strips of coloured paper to make paper chains, gathering bundles of ivy and other greenery from the woods near their Oxfordshire house – which would dry out and turn brown well before they were needed – and spending hours in the kitchen with her mother, covering herself in flour while she 'helped' to make the pastry, pressing out endless circles for the mince pies with a glass tumbler.

It pleased Laura to find that Holly was the same. She'd inspect the decorations Laura had put up with a critical eye, and change them about if they weren't completely to her liking. And she loved to cook, especially the baking. As soon as school, then college, had broken up, she would take over the kitchen and turn out mince pies, sausage rolls and cheese straws – until she got bored, of course, and disappeared to the village to reconnect with her friends, leaving Laura to clear up the mess and find enough tins and boxes in which to store all the food. No doubt it would be the same this year, when she came home from uni. Not that Laura was complaining. It was great that Holly showed an interest and, besides, you could never have too many mince pies.

This morning, then, Laura planned to pick up an extra couple of jars of homemade mincemeat from the WI market in preparation for Holly's marathon cook-in. She needed more Christmas cards, too – the bookshop always had a good selection.

And then there was Cynthia, the Christmas tree fairy, to be dealt with. Laura had bought the little plastic doll from Woolworths on hers and James's first Christmas together. She'd been dressed all in white with a silver wand and wings. James had taken one look and named her Cynthia. How he'd come up with the name she had no idea, but Cynthia she was, and that was that. As soon as Holly had been old enough to take notice, another tradition had been born – Cynthia must be freshly decked out every year. Grown up her daughter might be, but Laura would never get away with presenting Cynthia in last year's outfit.

Cynthia first, then, Laura decided, crossing the road as she turned into the high street. The wool shop, which had a good range of haberdashery, was one of her favourites. The narrow, black-and-white timbered building with the crooked roof was one of the oldest in Charnley Acre. It had a bowed window with glass so thick you had to peer closely to see what was on offer, and if you didn't duck as you went in, you were likely to receive a crack on the head from the low lintel. It all added to the charm, of course.

Pushing open the door, Laura ducked, and ran headlong into Clayton.

'Sorry,' he said, almost knocking a basket of wool off its stand as he stepped back. 'Oh, hello Laura. It's you.' He smiled.

'Yes, it's me.' Laura stood stupidly in the doorway, feeling wrong-footed at seeing him out of context. The wool shop seemed a strange place for Clayton to be.

Edging his way forward in the narrow space by the door, Clayton deftly reached behind Laura and released the door so that it swung shut. She had no option but to step forward herself, but Clayton didn't move, seemingly undecided whether he was staying or leaving. He seemed to find the whole dance-in-the-doorway thing amusing.

Laura laughed; she couldn't help herself. It came out as a girlish giggle but she decided to ignore that.

'Taken up knitting, have you?' she said, squeezing past the shelves of wool to enter the shop properly.

'Oh yes. I'm a regular little Kaffe Fassett. Didn't you know?' Clayton widened his eyes at her, the sensation of a smile beginning to show.

'You're winding me up.' Laura glanced at the balls of wool on the shelves. 'No pun intended.'

'None taken,' said Clayton. 'I'll hang on outside till you're done. I've got something to show you.'

'He's quite a character, isn't he?' remarked Veronica, the shop owner, giving Laura a wry look as she finally made it to the counter.

'Yes, I suppose he is.' Laura smiled distractedly, wondering what on earth Clayton could possibly have to show her.

She didn't have to wait to find out.

'He asked me to put this poster in the window.' Veronica held up a piece of A4 paper, printed in green and red, with the details of the Christmas tree sales. There was even a picture of a tree with a star on top. Clayton hadn't wasted any time there, had he?

'I must say it's *ever* so good of you to have the trees up at yours,' continued Veronica, leaning forwards across the counter, 'but if anybody was going to make amends, it'd be you.'

Make amends? Laura was confused for a moment, until she realised Veronica was referring to Spencer and his plans for the site. She sighed inwardly. She loved living in Charnley Acre, couldn't imagine living anywhere else, but nothing stayed private for long. Practically the whole village knew she was going out with Spencer, and now they knew about the change of venue for the Christmas trees, too. Which was right that they did, of course, if Clayton was to turn a decent profit. Out of the corner of her eye, she spotted one of his posters already taking pride of place in the window of the bakery across the road.

'Well, if it helps, then...' Laura tailed off. She wasn't going to start explaining herself. People could make of it what they liked.

She smiled. 'I've come about Cynthia. Her new outfit.' The Englebys' fairy was almost as well-known in the village as Laura herself. 'I thought pink this year. I found a bit of netting for the skirt, so I just need some pink ribbon to make the top, and a bit of pizazz of some sort.'

Veronica was already stooping below the counter. A long cardboard box was placed on top, the lid cast aside. 'Voila! My bits and pieces box. There'll be something in here. Cynthia was in blue last year, as I remember?'

'She was. Lavender the year before that, after the gold.'

Taking her time while she chatted to Veronica, Laura selected some wide, silky ribbon in deep rose pink to make the top half of the outfit, and a spool of silvery trimming to go around the skirt and the fairy's wings.

'You'll see how Cynthia looks when you come to the party,' Laura said, as Veronica rung up her purchases and put the items into a small paper bag. 'You are coming, you... and Jack?'

Veronica hesitated for a moment. She tucked a stray strand of silver-grey hair behind her ear, then smiled. 'Of course I'm coming. It's the highlight of Christmas! Not sure about Jack yet, but we'll see.'

Laura nodded. Every year, she'd invited Veronica and Jack to the party, and every year so far, Veronica had arrived alone. She seemed to enjoy herself, knowing most of the village as she did, and there was always someone on hand to see her home. Laura just let her be. Jack was a lovely man, from the little Laura knew of him, but he wasn't a mixer. She supposed that was the way he was and she didn't question it.

'Well, you're both very welcome,' she said, picking up the bag from the counter.

She'd been in the shop a while. With any luck, Clayton would have given up and gone by now. She could do without any further distraction today; her head seemed to be all over the place as it was.

But no, there he stood, studying the window display of the bookshop next door. Or perhaps pretending to. He smiled as she approached.

'I'm not lurking with intent. Or maybe I am. It's just that when I saw you I realised I should really have shown you these before I stuck them up all round the village, since they've got your address splashed all over them.' He lifted a fat yellow manila folder.

'The posters you mean? Veronica showed me hers, and it's fine. Just get on with whatever you need to do. You don't have to check in with me.'

Clayton tucked the folder beneath his arm. 'That's very good of you. Listen, I do appreciate this, especially, well...' He shrugged.

Laura smothered a smile. Clearly, Clayton still had Spencer on his mind as an integral part of their arrangement and it bothered him. She shouldn't have been surprised at his sensitivity though. Nothing he had ever said or done had yet revealed him to be the kind of man who didn't consider other people's feelings. Quite the reverse, in fact.

'Look, you really don't need to worry. I'm just happy that the trees will still be sold in Charnley Acre, or as near as,' she said.

One look at Clayton's face told her he understood what she was saying, despite neither of them having mentioned Spencer directly.

'Right, in that case, may I treat you to a coffee?' Clayton waved towards the Ginger Cat, a few shops along. 'I want to give them a poster anyway.'

So much for avoiding distraction, Laura thought. And Clayton was distracting, in quite an unnerving way; she'd only just admitted that to herself. But there, it was done now; she'd accepted his invitation, and they were seated at a table in the window of the Ginger Cat.

Half an hour later, coffee drunk and cartwheel-sized peanut butter cookies eaten, Clayton seemed in no hurry to leave. Talking to him was easy, the same as it was in her garden and at her kitchen table. There were some people, she was thinking, while Clayton relayed a funny tale about one of his gardening clients, that you felt you could say absolutely anything to and just be yourself. Clayton was one of them. Spencer, on the other hand... well, sometimes she felt she had to make a concerted effort, to look right, and to say the right thing.

Laura fiddled with an earring, her gaze fixed on the cats leaping around the rim of her plate. She was too eager to please, that was the trouble. Only last month she'd squeezed into a waist-clinching sapphire-blue silk dress and narrow sling-backs with pin-thin heels to attend a function with Spencer, and although he'd complimented her, and she knew it was just the kind of outfit he'd expected her to wear, she'd been mightily uncomfortable all evening. A little thing, okay, but little things added up, didn't they?

'Laura? Is everything all right?'

She looked up at Clayton. 'Yes, sorry. I just thought of something, that's all.'

He gave a firm little nod. 'You've got things to do. I mustn't hold you up any longer.'

At once, Clayton was up at the counter, paying at the till, and they were out in the street again.

The Saturday morning traffic streamed past, and amongst it, a dark-blue BMW.

CHAPTER 7

At first, Clayton thought Laura hadn't spotted Spencer swishing along the high street in that flash car of his. Then she'd performed a kind of double-take that she'd tried to cover up for his benefit, and he'd known otherwise. Blasted man seemed to be popping up everywhere these days.

He'd had to keep a strict watch on himself while they'd been having coffee in the Ginger Cat. For two pins he'd have told Laura, straight out, what kind of a man she was seeing – and who he really was. She was so easy to chat to that sometimes, while he was with her, he forgot to censor his thoughts as well as his words. He'd felt stupidly bereft when she'd said goodbye and gone off to finish her shopping.

But there, he'd be up at Spindlewood again on Monday for the winter trim and tidy. When Laura was out, he and Saul just got on with the gardening. She'd given him a key to the larger of the two sheds in case he wanted to use it. Therefore it didn't matter what time he turned up, but if he left Spindlewood until the last call on Monday, he'd stand a better chance of still being there when Laura came home from her school.

He hung about outside the bookshop to give her time to get

ahead of him before he, too, set off along the high street. Twenty minutes later, the manila folder was almost empty. Every shop had a poster, as had the library. The verger he'd met coming out of St Luke's churchyard had been happy to take one for the noticeboard in the church porch. He'd even foisted some on the WI ladies who were running the weekly market in the old village hall. There was also a new hall – well, newish – which formed part of the community centre, but that was on the outskirts of the village. He might call in there another time, when he had the van, in case there was anyone about. For now, it was home, and this afternoon he planned to tackle a job he'd been putting off for far too long.

As it happened, it wasn't until the evening when Clayton took a deep breath and prepared to knuckle down to his task. Had he been prevaricating again? Yes, that was part of it, but there had also been genuine reasons as to why he hadn't started earlier.

Arriving back at Mistletoe Cottage after his poster deliveries – and the pleasant time with Laura in the Ginger Cat – he'd found a large square parcel propped up against his front door, clearly addressed to his neighbour, Nell Whitby. It wasn't the first time he'd received post and parcels for her, and vice versa.

Nell lived at Mistlethrush Villa, one of a pair of handsome 1930's red-brick houses, four doors along. The delivery people were obviously in too much of a hurry to read the address properly, or couldn't be bothered, which was more like it. Dropping his folder on the doormat, he'd picked up the parcel and walked along with it. And then, of course, Nell had kept him chatting, but she was a nice woman – eighty-something, but full of life – and he hadn't minded.

What he *had* minded was the way she'd started on about

Christmas; the parcel apparently contained presents for her grandson. He'd hurried away then, as fast as he could without seeming rude.

As he'd let himself into his house, the phone had been ringing and, seeing Ruth Fielding's number on the little screen, he'd picked it up. Ruth was Saul's mother; the family lived in a converted barn on the outskirts of Charnley Acre. Before he'd moved into Mistletoe Cottage, Clayton had rented the barn's tiny annexe for a year and had become good friends with Ruth and her husband, Nathan. Ruth was calling now to ask him over for Sunday lunch tomorrow, an invitation Clayton easily accepted; she was a brilliant cook, and being in the Fieldings' company was always a pleasure, despite him spending almost every day with Saul.

Having ended the call from Ruth, various terminally boring, domestic tasks had pressed into his consciousness. The sun had decided to beam in through the windows and throw a spotlight on the half-inch of dust on the furniture, the cobwebs in the corners, and the dried tea stains on the kitchen worktops. Supposing, by some remote chance, he had a visitor? Normally he didn't make a show for visitors – they could take him as they found him – but in the back of his mind was Laura Engleby. Okay, there was no reason on earth why she should pay him a visit, but just supposing she did? Would he want her to find him living in a pigsty? Definitely not, even though she'd never pass judgement. And so, he'd got out the vacuum and the dusters and set to work, and before he knew it, the afternoon had raced away and it was dinner time.

Later, Clayton sat down at the cleared dining table, telling himself what a fool he was. Cleaning the cottage for an imaginary visitor – of course Laura wouldn't come – had been procrastination of the highest order. But now the time had arrived. If he didn't do this today, he never would. At least, that was how it felt.

In front of him was a large, flower-patterned box, bought by his sister, Louise, while she'd been living with him in Mistletoe Cottage. The box was temporary storage for her photographs, ready for when she had time to arrange them in the albums. He'd brought those down from Louise's old bedroom, too, where they'd lain untouched, like the box, for the past five years. Taking a deep breath, Clayton blew the dust off the lid, took it off and set it aside. He picked out a photo at random. Ironically, it was one he'd taken himself of Louise; he remembered grabbing the camera from her one day and taking the candid shot. His sister's lively hazel eyes smiled out at him and almost sent him reeling.

This was going to be really hard – that was even more apparent, now he'd started. In which case, why do it at all? Why torment himself unnecessarily?

Louise's passion for photography had given her much needed respite from her demanding job as a physiotherapist at Cliffhaven General. On her days off, she would drive for miles in search of likely subjects, and Clayton had sometimes gone with her. Birds were one of her favourites. Many a time he'd sat glued to a barren, windy spot on top of a cliff or the side of a hill, forbidden to move an inch while Louise clicked away at a swooping gull or fast-diving swallow. The harder the shot, the better she liked it. As he flicked through the perfectly captured frames of birds, as well as landscapes and seascapes, he was reminded how talented she was. Her photos deserved to be treated properly, however painful the task.

In the first place, then, he was doing this for Louise; it wasn't as if there was anything else he could do for her.

Secondly, there was something truly inspirational about Laura Engleby, something that gave him heart, and courage.

She'd been through the trauma of losing her partner but there she was, embracing life with an energy and purpose that almost shone from her. He wished she wasn't embracing Spencer – Marcus – at the same time, but perhaps it wasn't such a hopeless situation. If there was any justice in this world, Laura would discover the truth before it was too late.

Then again, if there was any justice, Marcus Dartnell would have gone down for manslaughter after he'd left Louise to die alone on a dark country road. Instead, he'd slithered away, like the evil snake he was, with a penalty for careless driving that was a pure insult.

Clayton got up, a little shakily, and went to the kitchen to fetch a glass of red wine. He brought it back to the table, then sat gazing at the picture of his sister before putting it aside and turning his attention back to the box.

CHAPTER 8

Veronica had been thinking about Laura Engleby's Christmas Eve party since she'd come into the shop for stuff to make the tree fairy's new outfit.

It was true that the legendary party at Spindlewood was the highlight of Christmas, unless you counted Boxing Day, when she and Jack went over to Lewes for dinner with her youngest cousin Hilary, her husband Mike, and their two daughters. The daughters might have boyfriends in tow, in fact, they usually did. Veronica thought one of the daughters had now moved out and set up home with a boyfriend. Yes, that was right; she remembered Hilary mentioning it in one of her endlessly long emails. Why she couldn't just pick up the phone Veronica didn't know. Anyway, Hilary was a marvellous cook and they'd have a nice time. They'd have to get taxis to and fro so that Jack could have a couple of beers, which was expensive, but that was all right.

Somehow, though, Boxing Day at Hilary's wasn't as much fun as Laura's party. The thing was, Veronica said to herself, as she tidied the shelves below the shop counter, the thing *was*, getting dressed up and going up to Spindlewood after dark made it seem like proper going out. It added a bit of excitement and glamour to the festive season. Veronica didn't do much *going out* these days. And as for excitement and glamour, you could forget it.

Evenings were spent mostly in front of the telly in their cottage in Mill Street, and she was content with that. Jack certainly was. If she wanted to see a film at the cinema down in Cliffhaven, he was willing to go with her, but they'd go to a matinee on the half day the shop shut, not in the evening. On the odd occasion – usually a birthday – when they went out for a meal, it would mean the early-bird sitting at the steak house when they'd be home by seven thirty, or Sunday lunch in a quiet pub off the beaten track.

Veronica didn't mean to sound ungrateful, even in private, inside her head, and she wasn't really. It was just that this year, she'd have liked them to turn up at Laura's as a couple, like other people did. And that, Veronica said to herself as she stood upright from the shelves, was as likely as spotting the proverbial pig flying past the window.

Jack didn't mind going to Hilary's. Or if he did, he'd never said. They hadn't been blessed with children, and they spent a peaceful Christmas Day at home, just the two of them. Jack approached Boxing Day with a brisk right-let's-get-this-over-with attitude but once he was there, he enjoyed himself in his own quiet way. He wasn't putting it on; Veronica would have known if he was, after all these years. The party at Spindlewood was a different kettle of fish entirely. Again, knowing him as she did, Veronica understood how he'd dread walking into a room full of people all laughing and talking and having a jolly time, even though he'd known most of them for years.

He never used to be like that, Veronica thought, as she stood behind the window display and gazed out at the street. Before he retired from the gas board, he'd been more outgoing, and remained so for a good while afterwards, until he'd sort of folded in on himself and no matter what she'd said or done, Veronica had never managed to unfold him.

He'd never been the life and soul – that wasn't his style – but he definitely used to be more sociable than he was now. The only place outside of home where he seemed comfortable was at the allotment. Sometimes, if Veronica wasn't in the brightest of moods, she'd accuse him of paying more attention to his cabbages than he did to her. And then a word or two would be exchanged, there'd be a bit of stomping about and the banging of a cupboard door or two until, by mutual, silent agreement, the mini-tiff was over and everything went back to normal.

Veronica wondered if Jack was depressed. She'd even talked him into going to the medical centre once, ages ago. She suspected he'd only agreed to stop her going on about it. But he hadn't let her go in with him. She'd had to sit in the waiting room, and when she asked him what the doctor had said, Jack had waved a prescription for antidepressants in front of her, then ripped it up and dropped it in the rubbish bin outside. She hadn't tried again.

But then, she couldn't complain, not really. Jack had a good heart, and he did care for her, she knew that. Other people had so much worse to deal with, and the world was a terrible place for so many. She was lucky.

But maybe she could broach the subject of the party again. Properly, not just asking casually if he wanted to go with her, then silently accepting his usual answer:

'No, ta. You go and have a good time, gal. You don't want me cramping your style.' Then he would wink, and go back to *Countdown*, or the news, or the crossword in the paper.

This year, Veronica wanted a different answer, and somehow she would get it.

CHAPTER 9

It was half past eleven on Sunday morning. Saul Fielding lay fully dressed on top of his unmade bed, gazing up at the miserable grey skies through the skylight. He'd already been up for hours. He'd surprised his family – and himself – by appearing downstairs at half past eight and demolishing a fair old stack of pancakes with blueberries and maple syrup for breakfast. Carbs, of course, were the best hangover cure known to man; it had been worth the effort to drag himself out of bed.

Now, though, his whole body had begun to protest about its rude awakening in every way possible. Levering himself up and lurching to one side, he fumbled in the bedside drawer and located by feel a squashed packet of paracetamol. Last night's water stagnated in the glass; it would have to do. Swallowing two tablets with the water, Saul made an 'urgh' sound, and flopped onto his back.

This extra rest time was essential if he was going to appear *compos mentis* by lunchtime. There'd be no getting away with it. Mum and Dad made a big thing about the family eating together, especially Sunday lunch when it was always a roast.

Mum was a fab cook, though, and Dad wasn't at all bad at conjuring up his speciality, Yorkshire pudding. Saul wouldn't have any trouble getting stuck in.

Clayton was coming to lunch, apparently. It seemed a bit sad, a man of Clayton's age living alone and having to cook for himself all the time. That wouldn't happen to Saul. No way. But life had a habit of kicking you in the teeth, as it must have done to Clayton. Saul didn't know the details but he did know he'd had a serious girlfriend a while back until it had all gone arse upwards. And then he'd been dealt another blow when he'd lost his sister in that tragic way, which was just about the cruellest thing you could think of. Saul's kid sister, Katy, might be a permanent pain in the butt, but he'd be devastated if anything like that happened to her, or to any of his family.

Saul sighed. Who knew how life would turn out? Perhaps he would end up on his own. Just think of that. Saul thought; he didn't like it much. Which brought his mind neatly back to his current preoccupation. Girls. Or *girl*, if you wanted to be picky about it. The thing was, knowing how shitty life could get made you realise you shouldn't prat about wasting precious time. If you wanted something – or some*one* – you should just go for it, which was exactly what he intended to do, as soon as she came home for the Christmas holidays.

Holly Engleby.

He'd known her like forever – her family had lived in Charnley Acre almost as long as his – but only in the way that he'd seen her around the village, with other kids, and at birthday parties and stuff. They hadn't been at school together because she'd gone to an all-girls' school, otherwise they might have been proper friends. She'd been a regular at the youth club, same as him, but even then he hadn't clocked how wonderful she was. Too busy smoking illicit fags round the back of the hall, probably.

Then, once they'd all kind of grown up, there she was, all golden-blonde hair and big blue-grey eyes, like a shining new star that had just come out in the sky. Other girls he'd fancied – been out with, in some cases – had seemed to fade away into the background. She'd got flirty with him, sometimes, but everyone flirted with everyone else. It didn't mean a lot – it was just what you did – but he couldn't ignore the way Holly seemed to single him out. It was his bad luck that just as he'd been working his way up to asking her out on a proper date instead of just messing about in a crowd, she'd taken herself off to Birmingham uni to study English Literature or something.

She'd come home for a week in October, which was when it had truly begun. With the cold weather closing in, the Goose and Feather had become the regular hang-out spot – it wasn't like there was anywhere else to go if you wanted to keep it local – and Holly had been there, almost every night. The Goose had a back room with a pool table, and mostly everyone gravitated out there.

Even when they were amongst the crowd, having a laugh, sometimes he'd felt like it was just the two of them. He'd hoped Holly felt that way too. All the signs that she did were there: the private smiles she gave him from across the room; the way she'd appear by his side when he went to the bar and they'd talk for a while, before they rejoined the others.

And then, on her last night – his heart rate increased as the memory flooded in – they'd gone for a wander in the dark, down the lane that ran alongside the pub, and, naturally, they'd had a bit of a snogging session. Well, more than a bit, as it went. He'd known then for absolute certain that she really liked him.

They'd already had each other's numbers in their phones, because everyone did, and once she'd gone back to uni, he'd texted her a couple of times right away, just jokey stuff, and she'd texted back a few words each time. It wasn't much to go on but it was enough to give him hope that when she came home for the Christmas holidays, they'd pick up where they'd left off.

It had felt like a total gift – a bloody miracle – when he'd found out he'd be spending three whole weeks in Holly's garden. He could have kissed her mother. Well, no, he couldn't – that would be seriously weird. He'd leave that to Clayton who, if Saul wasn't hugely mistaken, was well up for the task. He'd seen the way Clayton looked at Laura Engleby, like he couldn't take his eyes off her. And again, if he wasn't mistaken, Laura was the same with Clayton. Pity she was going out with that posh bloke who drove the BMW, but that needn't be an obstacle, providing everything else was right.

Saul chuckled to himself. Right on cue, he heard the unmistakable noise of the Green and Fragrant van pulling up outside. Getting up from the bed, he bounded downstairs.

Saul had left his car in the village last night. He'd totally forgotten about that until he happened to glance out of the window during lunch and noticed that his usual parking space in front of the house was empty. His fault, of course, for having been too idle to walk to his mate George's house in the first place. There'd been a bit of a gathering there because George's parents were away for the weekend. It hadn't been that great, actually; all sitting about and nothing much to do except drink. He couldn't wait until Holly came home, then he'd have more exciting nights out to look forward to.

Everyone sat around after lunch, reading the Sunday papers and chatting, apart from Katy, who was in the den with one of her mates, playing some annoyingly squeaky computer game. Around three, Clayton made a move to leave, and Saul took the chance to blag a lift to George's house to collect his car.

Clayton was quiet at the start of the journey, quieter than usual. Not that there was a lot to say, seeing as they were together most days anyway. As they drove down the hill, they passed Spindlewood, and Saul noticed a slowing of the van as Clayton took a hard look towards the gates.

'What're you smiling at?' Clayton said, speeding up again.

'Oh, nothing.' Saul smothered the grin.

Actually, this might be a good time to gather a little advice.

'Do you think long-distance relationships can ever work?' he said, trying to sound dead casual.

'I don't know, I've never tried one,' Clayton said. 'I guess it depends on whether the feelings between the people concerned are strong enough. Why? Ah, hang on. This wouldn't be anything to do with the toothsome Holly Engleby, would it?'

Now it was Clayton's turn to grin. Saul wished he hadn't asked. What sort of a word was *toothsome*, anyway?

'Not necessarily,' he said, feigning nonchalance. 'I'm talking theoretically.'

'Theoretically.'

'Yes, I said.' Saul looked at Clayton's amused expression in the mirror, and sighed. 'Okay, yes. Holly. Have it your way.'

Clayton slowed the van as they rounded the bend and entered the high street before he answered. 'You do know she'll have loads of opportunities while she's at university? And I don't need to tell you what sort of opportunities. As will you, when you start agricultural college.'

'That's not till next September, and in any case I'll be living at home. It's hardly the same thing. So, you're saying that, like, even if she's really into me it won't stop her looking elsewhere?'

'I'm not saying she would. I know nothing about her. But unless you're in a committed relationship, it's on the cards, isn't it? Sorry, I don't want to pour cold water on your romantic ambitions but...'

'Yeah, yeah, it's cool.' Already Saul had had enough of this conversation. It was starting to get embarrassing. 'Forget I said anything.'

'She's a lovely girl, though,' Clayton said. 'I'm not surprised you like her.'

'And I'm not surprised you like her mother.'

He could have bitten that back. Since when did he discuss his employer's love life – or lack of – with him? But Clayton didn't seem in the least bit fazed. He just laughed, which told Saul one hell of a lot more than if he'd answered directly.

'Where's this car of yours then?'

'Turn left by the church, up Caburn Street, then it's a sharp right. What're we doing tomorrow?'

'Couple of pruning jobs at Kingston, then over to Ringmer to plant some new shrubs. I'll pick you up at ten by the bus stop. Later on, it's Spindlewood but I can do that on my own, otherwise it'll mean you hanging about in the meantime.'

Saul could have asked why they couldn't go straight on to Spindlewood from the previous job and avoid any *hanging about*. He didn't though. Sometimes it was best not to push it.

CHAPTER 10

'I'm sorry, Laura, but I've got to say this. I want you to cancel the Christmas tree arrangement. In fact, I don't want you to have any more to do with Clayton Masters.'

Laura spun round and stared at Spencer, hardly able to believe what she'd heard. It was Saturday evening and they were in Spencer's over-designed kitchen. He'd been stirring the sauce for their pasta supper when suddenly he'd dropped the spoon into the pan and turned to her.

'What on *earth* are you talking about?' Laura put her hands to her mouth, and instinctively stepped further back from Spencer. 'You know I can't cancel. The trees are being delivered on Monday, ready to be sold from Tuesday on. And why shouldn't I have anything to do with Clayton? You're not making any sense.'

It was one thing, Spencer not getting on with Clayton, but to tell her – no, *order* her – to cut away from him altogether was beyond ridiculous. What had got into him?

They'd had a lovely day. They'd driven to Ashdown Forest and walked on springy turf amongst the heather in bright sunshine, well wrapped up in coats and scarves against the cold.

They'd eaten a delicious lunch in a pub with a roaring fire in the inglenook and a Christmas tree in the corner, and now they were back at Spencer's mock-Georgian house, all set for a relaxing evening in front of the TV.

Or so she'd thought.

Spencer let out a sigh that stopped just short of impatient. 'I've been wanting to say something all day but I didn't want to spoil things.'

Laura threw him a challenging look. 'You knew how I'd react then? Well, I'm sorry for being so predictable.'

'Laura, I do wish you'd try to understand my feelings in all of this.'

His feelings? What about hers?

'All of *what*? Spence, how can I understand when I've got no idea why you feel so strongly about Clayton? What's he done to you, apart from oppose the plans for the housing development? That was just business, you said so yourself. I was surprised it got so out of hand in the pub that night...'

'You weren't there, Laura. Nothing got out of hand. You know what the village gossips are like for exaggerating.'

'Well, according to Emily, you put on quite a show. I must say I was surprised at both of you.'

Spencer's eyes blazed. 'Oh well, if Emily said so, then it *must* be true.'

What?

'Spencer, stop this, *please*.' Laura's hands had curled themselves into tight fists. She moved a few steps nearer to him. He was worrying her now. She toned down her voice, speaking more gently. 'What's wrong? Is work stressing you out or something?'

'I'm fine. Work's not the problem.'

Ah, so there *was* a problem, one she was so far unaware of. Laura thought back to the other day when she'd decided she'd been trying too hard to please Spencer. Problem or not, he wasn't getting his own way this time.

'If you won't tell me what it is, I can't help, can I?' she said.

Spencer pinched the bridge of his nose. He looked tired, but a shadow of anger still darkened his features. Anger that she had no idea how to deal with. Edging past him, she switched off the hotplate; the sauce had started to congeal. Turning back to him, she tentatively held out her hand. He ignored it.

'Spence, this has all got out of proportion. Okay, so you fell out with Clayton over the site development, and besides that, it's obvious you don't particularly like him. Goodness knows why, but fair enough – we can't like everybody, all of the time. But he happens to be my gardener, and he's a damn good one at that. The Christmas tree thing is simply another bit of business between us. I've let him have the use of a slice of my garden – for which he is paying me, in case you were wondering – but it's only for three weeks. And then it'll be Christmas, and that will be lovely, won't it? Aren't you looking forward to Christmas, my party and everything? I know I am.'

To her own ears, Laura sounded as if she was talking to a child, but Spencer deserved that because he was being childish. He looked at her for a long moment, then turned and walked out of the kitchen. She followed him through to the living room. Perhaps if they sat down, and Spencer relaxed, they could sort this out quickly and move on. But he didn't sit down. Instead he paced to the front window and pulled the cord to close the curtains, then stood in the bay, facing the room. He seemed stiff, ill at ease with himself. Again, Laura worried about what it might mean, never mind the demands he was making of her. A dragging sense of déjà vu suffused her, from the night she'd run out on their dinner date.

'If you must know,' he said heavily, 'Clayton Masters and I

have got history. And please don't ask me what it is because it's private.'

Private? Laura had thought they were close, close enough to confide in one another, surely? How could he keep something like that a secret from her, especially when it directly involved her?

She stood behind a red leather armchair, resting her hands on its back, facing Spencer.

'But that's ridiculous. How can you expect me to do as you ask when you won't tell me why? It's not on, Spence. Surely you can see that.'

'Laura, I *said* don't ask me, and I meant it. It's not something I want to talk about, ever.' Spencer sounded exasperated now, on the point of losing it completely. 'Can't you just trust me on this and tell Clayton the deal's off? The bloody Christmas trees are *not* your problem.'

'No,' Laura said. 'I can't and I won't. Whatever it is, you'll have to get over it. Sorry.'

Sorry? She had nothing to apologise for. Her boyfriend, on the other hand, was chalking up unspent apologies by the minute.

Spencer took a step towards her. 'He isn't just your gardener, though, is he?'

'What do you mean?' Laura's insides quaked. Please God she wasn't blushing, because something deep inside was edging her towards it, as if she had something to feel guilty about.

'I saw the pair of you sitting in the window of the Ginger Cat last Saturday morning. You were having a very cosy chat by the looks of it.'

Laura almost laughed. 'So, you saw us having coffee. Well, so what? I'm not going to tell you how that came about because, quite honestly, it's none of your business.'

Hang on, he'd said he'd seen them inside the Ginger Cat,

when she had only seen Spencer driving by once they'd come outside. Which meant he must have driven past twice, at least.

'Were you checking up on me?' she said, narrowing her eyes at him.

'No, of course I wasn't. I happened to be passing. But seeing you socialising with him underlines what I'm saying now. Clayton is not the kind of man you should be associating with, and I'm telling you that for your own good. If you loved me, you'd do what I ask.'

Laura's fingers dug into the leather of the chair. Waves of heat undulated through her body, setting her face on fire. 'If I loved you, I'd do anything for you without question? Is that it?'

'No, not *anything*. Just this one thing. You're twisting my words.'

Laura stayed silent, looking down at the chair back that now had a series of dents in it from the pressure of her fingernails. Was she being unreasonable, expecting Spencer to explain what he meant about there being history between him and Clayton? Shouldn't she simply trust him, as he said? Give him the benefit of the doubt, the same as she hoped he would do for her?

She looked up at him. He'd relaxed his stance, lowered his shoulders. But the firm set of his chin and his unwavering gaze told her he wasn't going to relent. Well, neither was she. It would be wrong, let alone impossible. They'd reached an impasse. So, now what? It seemed it was up to her to try and smooth things over. Either that or pick up the argument and watch their relationship spiral out of control, as it almost had done already.

She rounded the chair and made a move towards him. To her relief, he met her halfway. His arms went around her. She kept her arms by her side but let him hold her. He kissed her forehead.

'Laura, I didn't mean to upset you. I've so enjoyed being with you today. It's been great, hasn't it?'

His voice held a note of appeal. But she had to stay strong. She sighed. 'I had a lovely day too, and I wish you hadn't...' She'd been going to say she wished he hadn't ruined it, but that wouldn't have been helpful.

'Spence, I have to stand by what I believe is right. And what is right, for me, is that I carry on employing Clayton to do the garden and let him sell the trees from Spindlewood. So yes, I will be seeing more of him than usual for those few weeks, and I'm truly sorry if that offends you but there really isn't anything I can do about that.'

She almost added, 'and if you don't like it you can stay away,' but she didn't. Instead, she smiled to temper her words. And then, after a moment, she kissed him, and his return kiss spoke of normality. They broke apart.

'Let's drop the subject for now,' Spencer said.

No, not *for now*, Laura, thought. Let that be an end to it once and for all. But she said nothing more, except to ask him to run her home, because at that moment, home was where she wanted to be. Alone.

'I can't imagine how he had the nerve to ask you that. I mean, *why*, for heaven's sake?'

Emily gazed around her in disbelief, as if the answer would jump out of the bushes at any moment. Laura wished it would, because it certainly wasn't coming from anywhere else.

'I know. It's crazy, isn't it? I don't know what to do.'

Emily shot Laura a sideways look. 'Surely you aren't considering giving in to Spencer? He has to know he can't run your life, and he definitely has no right to tell you who you can or can't see.'

'Which is what I told him last night, more or less. Em, I've no intention of giving in to him, and even if I had, it's too late to stop the Christmas trees being delivered to my house. What I mean is, I don't know what to do about Spencer, our relationship. How to bring this back.'

Emily blew out air. 'I'd have thought that was up to him. It's his fault. He's the one who has to make the running, not you. How was it when you left him last night?'

Laura thought for a moment. 'It was okay – on the surface anyway. He didn't ask to come in when he dropped me home but we had a goodnight kiss. He didn't mention Clayton again, not on the way home or when we got there, and neither did I. He said he'd call me today. I didn't have the heart to tell him not to bother.'

They'd followed the public footpath that ran alongside Cloud Cottage, Emily's home, and were now at the gate which opened onto Charnley Common. Emily stooped to detach Wilf's lead from his harness. The dog sniffed the air and loped off across the grass, heading straight for a small white terrier which was bouncing around on the end of a long lead. The terrier's owner, a grey-haired woman in a pink anorak, gave a wave. Emily waved back.

They strolled on a little way before Emily resumed the conversation. 'Spencer's the one in the wrong and he knows it.'

'But that's just it,' Laura said. 'He's got no idea he's in the wrong. He thinks I'm the one who's being unreasonable, he made that pretty clear. For all I know he may have a point. Perhaps I should have taken it at face value and trusted him. Whatever's gone on between him and Clayton in the past, it must be pretty serious for him to make all this fuss, mustn't it?'

'Not so serious that he can't share it with you, Laura. You say you should have trusted him. Well, what about him trusting you? Share and share alike. Isn't that what relationships are all about?'

Emily darted off to peel Wilf away from the terrier. Laura stood still, gazing across the common into the distance where the mist threw a gauze shroud over the bare black branches of the trees. She'd puzzled half the night over Spencer's revelation that he and Clayton had 'history'. She couldn't even begin to guess what it might be about. It proved one thing, though; she'd been right about there being more to their disagreement than the development plans. But, as Emily said, why make a mystery out of it? If Spencer wanted to win her over, then why not bolster his case by telling her the whole story?

Her phone vibrated in her pocket. She took it out and looked at the screen. Spencer. He'd called her half an hour ago; she hadn't heard it. Now there was a text: *Where are you? Can we talk please? I love you x*. He must have called the landline at the house too, then.

Emily was back, and saw Laura looking at her phone.

'Is that him?'

'Yep.' Laura switched the phone off and slid it back into her pocket, walking on to catch up with her friend. 'Well, he can wait. I'm not in the mood to talk to him.'

'Neither would I be,' Emily said. 'He doesn't deserve you if he's going to behave like that.'

Laura laughed. 'Or, looking at it another way, maybe he does. I can be a stroppy mare at times.'

Emily laughed too. 'This is true, but only when you're pushed. Seriously though, Laura, is Spencer *the one*, the one after lovely James, I mean?'

'I thought so, I really did. He's gorgeous and sexy, and he's kind and thoughtful,' – she pulled a face – 'well, usually.'

'And you are still in love with him?' Emily's golden-brown eyes narrowed, the way they did when she wanted a serious answer to a serious question.

'Yes, of course I am,' Laura said quickly.

It felt like an automatic response, which alarmed her slightly. She trod down hard on the feeling before it could take hold.

Emily gave her a long look before she said, 'You know, there might be a way to find out what's gone on between Spencer and Clayton. If Spencer's not playing the game, then ask Clayton what it's all about.'

'I couldn't do that! We're not on those kind of terms. It would be like prying into his personal affairs. Anyway, he'd know Spencer hadn't told me and he'd wonder why.'

'Yeah, I guess. Talking of affairs, though, who's he seeing? Clayton, I mean. I won't believe it if you tell me he hasn't been snapped up.'

Laura laughed again. She might not be any further forward, but Emily was such a tonic. She'd been right to seek her out this morning. She felt so much better already.

'If you must know, he hasn't. Clayton is single. At least that's what he told me.'

'You asked him? So you *are* on those kinds of terms then.' Emily was triumphant.

Laura suppressed a grin. 'If you'll shut up a minute...' She recounted her conversation with Clayton, when she'd invited him to her Christmas Eve party.

Actually, he'd been pretty evasive about that, she remembered. Well, of course he would have been, because he knew Spencer would be there. It all made sense now. Pity though. She'd have loved Clayton to come to her party. A thought struck her.

'Are you planning on seducing my gardener?' she said to Emily.

'Nope. Sorry to disappoint. I can see the attraction for others but he does nothing for me, not in that way.'

For some reason, Laura was pleased to hear it.

Emily suddenly gave a piercing, two-fingered whistle that had Laura backing away in protest.

'Wilf's getting deafer,' Emily said. 'Which is why my whistle's getting louder. *Wilf!*'

The dog raised his head from the rabbit hole he'd been sniffing around and cantered obediently back to Emily.

'I need coffee,' she said, reattaching Wilf's lead.

As they reached Cloud Cottage and passed through the wrought-iron gate into Emily's small front garden, Laura remembered something. She put a hand on Emily's arm.

'Hey, you haven't told me how the date went?'

'It never happened. That's why.'

Emily took her keys out of her pocket and Laura followed her round to the back door; the front one was hardly ever used.

'What d'you mean, it never happened?' Laura said, pausing to use the rusty boot-scraper before following Emily into the kitchen.

Emily filled the kettle and switched it on. She let out a sigh, a regretful one, Laura thought. Her heart went out to her friend. She so deserved to meet somebody nice.

'I drove all the way to Worthing to meet him halfway from where he lives, only to get a ruddy text message saying he'd met somebody else online and decided to pursue that contact instead. Honestly, "pursue that contact"! What a way to put it!' Emily sighed again. 'Pity though. He was one of the few men over forty-five who don't expect to hook up with a twenty-one-year-old.'

'Even so...' Laura said, thinking that her friend was well out of that one.

'Not my type? No, I don't suppose he would've been. I might have another crack at the site tonight.'

'He's out there somewhere, your perfect man.'

'I'd settle for semi-perfect,' Emily said. Then, with a twinkle in her eye, she added, 'Even semi-detached.'

Laura laughed. 'You don't mean that.'

'Don't I?'

Emily's oak-beamed, yellow-painted kitchen was warm and cosy and inviting. Laura sank into a chair at the oilcloth-covered table and realised how tired she was, not just from her restless night but from the constant niggling worries about the Spencer-Clayton thing. She rubbed at her gritty eyes.

'You look knackered,' Emily observed.

'Cheers for that.'

'You're welcome. I would say stay for the rest of the day but I'm going ice skating with the guys.'

She meant her colleagues at *Cliffhaven News*, Laura knew. She also knew they weren't all guys, but, unfortunately for Emily, those who were either had wives or girlfriends, or were too young, even for her.

'It's okay, I've got things to do. I'll toddle off in a minute. I want to make my food list for the Christmas Eve party, then sort out the tree decorations. And Cynthia awaits her new outfit. I bought some bits and bobs for her from Veronica.'

Not long afterwards, Laura jumped into her car, waving back at Emily who was standing in the doorway of her pretty thatched cottage, mouthing silent words and gesticulating like mad. Laura interpreted all this to mean she was to text Emily later with an update on the Spencer situation. She was laughing as she drove off.

But as she turned the car into the high street and drove past the Ginger Cat, her mood dipped again. She didn't want Spencer to be miserable because of her, and if she had unwittingly caused that, then she was truly sorry. All this was casting a shadow over Christmas. The coming weeks should be exciting and festive. Holly was coming home. There were preparations to be made for the party, and for Christmas Day, when her mum, Rachael, Rachael's husband, Paul, and their two daughters, would make up the usual family gathering. There was the Christmas pageant at school to look forward to, which was hard work but always lovely. And this year, there would be the added fun of the Christmas trees in her garden, and half the village turning up to buy them.

Laura slammed the gears unintentionally hard. *Damn Spencer*. Emily was right; this was all down to him – she'd done nothing wrong. How could he even think of spoiling this special time of year when he knew how much it meant to her? It was too bad of him, it really was.

CHAPTER 11

The children in Laura's teaching group were always hyperactive on a Monday morning. After two days of not seeing one another, she had to shout to be heard above the clamour of voices and the squeak of chairs on the rubber floor of the classroom. Today was no exception, but she'd made it ten times worse by raising the subject of the Christmas pageant.

Robyn and Rosie, nine-year-old twins with Down's, shrieked in delight and high-fived each other when Laura confirmed that yes, they could both be angels, and *yes*, they could wear pink dresses, *and* have pink wings. She crossed her fingers at this point and hoped the costume team could fulfil this dream.

A bit of a to-do broke out as Thomas, a solemn child, full of detailed knowledge about the weirdest of subjects, stood up and informed the class that angels *never* wore pink, they only wore white, because angels came from Heaven, where everything was white, or gold. Undeterred, the twins started another round of high-fives which spread around the classroom like fire on a dry heath until Laura threatened that none of them would be in the pageant unless they were quiet and sat still, *now*.

But inside she was laughing, and loving them all, because

they were loveable, every one of them, from the most exuberant, like Robyn and Rosie, and across the scale to a pale little boy called Simon, who frequently vanished into his own secret world from which nobody could prise him until he was ready.

Later in the morning, Laura bundled into her duffle coat and scarf, and went outside to the grassed play area, leaving her teaching assistant, Clare, holding a chaotic music session with the kids. Crossing to the far side of the green, she sat on one of the logs the children liked to sit and climb on. There was no sun, but it wasn't especially cold. Beneath a blank white sky, the air had the kind of perfect stillness that only came in the depths of winter. Looking up, Laura wondered if it would snow this year. A white Christmas would be marvellous; there hadn't been one of those for a long time.

It had been snowing when she'd first met Spencer. It was almost two years ago, not at Christmas but at the end of January. She'd been to a jeweller's in Lewes to buy a silver bracelet for Holly's birthday, and the jeweller had offered to engrave it the same day if she wanted to come back in an hour. She had passed the time by wandering around the shops, and then, because it had suddenly turned bitingly cold, she'd nipped into the town hall where there was an exhibition of architectural designs for ongoing Sussex projects. Reps from building and architectural companies were roaming the thin crowd, ready to answer questions.

Laura had been gazing at the drawings for the renovation of a Jacobean manor house when she'd felt a presence and, turning, she'd seen Spencer, gazing at her as openly as she'd been gazing at the drawings. It had been love at first sight – well, lust at first sight was probably more accurate. They'd begun chatting, as naturally as if they were old friends, until Laura had looked up at the high window and seen a myriad snowflakes whirling and dancing out of a slate-grey sky.

She'd have been fine going home, of course – the snow had hardly begun to settle – but Spencer had sweetly insisted on accompanying her back to the jeweller's to pick up the bracelet, and then he'd followed her all the way home, his car trailing hers as if it was glued to her bumper. Just to make sure she got home safely, he'd said, since he lived in the same village. He'd have done the same had he lived miles away in the other direction; she'd known that as well as he had. On their arrival at Spindlewood, she'd parted with her phone number after only a brief hesitation.

She'd dated on and off over the years since James had died, but nobody had made her feel the way Spencer had. She'd been scared to look forward and, suddenly, the future had seemed full of exciting possibilities.

Laura thought about yesterday. Arriving home from Emily's, she'd found Spencer's car parked in front of the house, the man himself standing beside it with an anxious look on his face and his dark hair all rumpled. The rush of love she'd experienced at the sight of him had knocked everything else into perspective. Before the feeling had had a chance to dissipate, she'd apologised, firstly for not taking his call this morning, and then for anything she might have done or said to upset him. Spencer had held his hands up in protest. No, *he* was one who was sorry, and he would make it up to her, if she'd forgive him for being such an idiot.

Remembering Emily's words, Laura had wavered, but not for long. Nobody was perfect – she certainly wasn't – and Spencer had cared enough to seek her out. It crossed her mind that guilt might have played a part in this impromptu visit, but she'd decided to ignore that. She'd invited him in, pleased that he hadn't presumed she would, and the rest of the day had passed in relaxed, Sunday-ish fashion. Then day turned to night, and Laura had wanted Spencer to stay as much as he clearly did.

It had been past midnight when she had slipped out of bed, taking care not to wake Spencer, and sent Emily a brief text – the thumbs-up sign and two red hearts.

Spencer had left after breakfast, with a promise to phone her tonight. After his initial apology, not a word had been said about their argument, nor Clayton or the Christmas trees. By rights, she shouldn't have felt grateful for that – apologies and a night of passion or not, Spencer still owed her an explanation – but grateful was exactly how she'd felt.

It was peace, of a sort, although already it felt fragile, the slivers of doubt in her mind chipping away at the surface.

The cacophony from her class's music session had died down and now the long, shrill note of the school bell signalled lunchtime. Laura got up from the log and walked towards her classroom. This afternoon, after the reading lesson, she'd get the class to make snowflakes out of paper doilies to decorate the windows. It would be noisy and messy but a nice Christmassy afternoon was exactly what she needed.

Emily arrived home from work a little after seven on Monday evening, having put in a nine-hour day. She didn't mind the unsocial hours so much in the summer but at this time of year the lanes around Charnley Acre became twisting black tunnels after dark, and you had to drive extra slowly and watch for the headlights of oncoming traffic. The temperature had dropped suddenly tonight, too, and the twiggy tops of the bare hedgerows already sparkled with a dusting of frost.

She made a fuss of Wilf, who'd risen stiffly from his bed to greet her. Putting a match to the log-burner and switching on the lamps soon made the living room bright and cosy, and Emily brought her supper through to have on a tray by the fire.

As she ate, she thought about Christmas. It would have been nice not to be alone again this year, but there, you couldn't have everything. Not that she'd be alone in the literal sense – she'd be at her parents' sprawling Victorian house in Brighton, which would be packed to the cornices with aunts and uncles, nephews and nieces, and family friends who had been around so long that they were as good as family anyway. She was lucky, she knew that; there were plenty of people who had nobody at all to spend the festive season with.

That first Christmas after the divorce, Emily had felt nothing but the utmost relief at being single and free. She'd let out a long, metaphorical sigh, and then it was as if she'd become as light as a feather, winging her way through the festivities like a manic Christmas fairy. But that was three years ago, and since then, none of her dates had come up to the mark, which, to be fair, was probably mutual in most cases.

Emily's eyes alighted on the laptop, sitting across the room on the gateleg table, its lid up in readiness. Did she have the energy, or the will, to give it another go tonight? That was the question. It was only three weeks until Christmas; three weeks until Laura's party. She wouldn't be the only guest without a partner, far from it, but that wasn't the point. The point was that she would rather arrive with somebody, and leave with the same person, than act the part of the happy-go-lucky singleton all evening. Then she wouldn't have to run the gauntlet of the rubbish selection of unattached blokes from the village who seemed to think she was fair game for a chat-up. It wasn't only the single ones who hit on her either. Last year, a man she knew only by sight had leaned across from his seat after the briefest of small talk and said into her ear, none too quietly, that he'd really like to kiss her, on the lips.

'That's not going to happen, is it?' she'd said frostily, glancing pointedly at the man's wife who was sitting at the other side of him.

Sometimes she wondered where Laura dredged up some of these party guests. No, that wasn't fair; Emily retracted the thought. It was due to Laura's love of Christmas and her generous nature that so many turned up to her party, and the more the merrier, as far as Laura was concerned.

No doubt Spencer would be there, which was lovely for Laura, of course, although now, seeing her friend so confused and angry about what had happened on Saturday night, she wasn't as sure as she used to be that Spencer was right for her. And then there was the altercation he'd had with Clayton in the Goose. Everyone Emily had spoken to said it was Spencer who'd goaded Clayton and turned the thing into a pitch battle, and she had no reason to disbelieve them. She hadn't mentioned that part to Laura, of course. It would have seemed too much like telling tales against Laura's boyfriend. She'd recounted the basic story, and that was all Laura had needed to know.

Emily set down her tray with its empty plate on the footstool. The meal had revived her enough for her to move across to the table and fire up the laptop. While she waited for the site to load, she took her mobile from her pocket and scrolled to the message Laura had sent in the middle of last night. A thumbs up and two hearts could only mean that she and Spencer were all loved up again, and everything was rosy in Paradise. Emily had smiled when she'd seen it; now it seemed almost too good to be true, as if they'd made up too quickly. Then again, if Spencer had now told Laura the full story about this mysterious 'history' he had with Clayton, and it sounded reasonable, maybe she was worrying about her friend unnecessarily.

The entwined hearts logo appeared on the computer screen. Emily entered her password. The hearts performed a little jive.

No matches or messages. Oh yes, there was one, from yet another bloke who could hardly string two words together, never mind spell them correctly. She was no intellectual snob, but really, she drew the line at men who couldn't spell. Emily made a face at the screen. She was tempted to add a rider to her profile: *Strangers to the written word need not apply*.

Okay, so not this one then. She loaded up another site, one she'd only recently joined. The tone of it had seemed a bit stiff and formal before, but now, looking again at the words 'mature professionals' it seemed she might have misjudged it. She was a professional, wasn't she? And as for mature, well, if you took that to mean you wouldn't see forty again and you had a level-headed grip on life, she might possibly qualify after all. As long as the blokes who'd signed up to this one weren't positively ancient and their profiles weren't complete works of fiction, her soulmate could be a few clicks away.

Emily scrolled. Fifteen minutes later, she was still scrolling and speed-reading. A media type caught her eye. His profile said he was fifty-two – eight years older than her – but he looked good on it. More scrolling. A company director smiled out at her quite appealingly. It didn't say what sort of company but she supposed that wasn't relevant. Another fifteen minutes, and Emily had registered her interest against three possibles. She laughed. The triumph of hope over experience; that about summed it up.

She glanced at the clock. It was almost ten. A few minutes more, then she'd pack it in and pop Wilf out for his last walk. Scrolling again, a familiar face appeared, causing her to draw in a sharp breath. The man on the screen had dark hair cropped short on top, and wore rimless glasses pushed down slightly over his nose, the way some men wore them when they wanted to look intellectual. Despite the slight differences, the face was unmistakeable, but the name attached to the photo wasn't

Spencer Jennings, it was Marcus Dartnell. Emily examined the photo again, peering closely at the screen. The man she knew didn't wear glasses, but he could have contact lenses, and hair changed all the time. No, she hadn't been mistaken, it was definitely Laura's boyfriend.

Right, time for some logical thinking here. Emily sat back in her chair and narrowed her eyes at the screen. The man in the photo looked slightly younger than the one she knew. According to his profile, he was forty-four and his location was given as Gloucestershire, not Sussex. Had Laura once mentioned that Spencer used to live in Gloucestershire? It seemed to ring a faint bell. So, this was an old listing, that must be it. He'd forgotten he'd signed up, or just never bothered to take his profile down, and wasn't receiving alerts for any matches he got.

He hadn't updated his location, which was reassuring. It seemed to indicate that he hadn't been in the market for a new girlfriend while he was seeing Laura. There was no reason to panic then. And no reason, either, to say a word to Laura about what she'd found, not right now anyway. What purpose would it serve? So, Spencer had signed up to a dating site before he met Laura, using a different name. That wasn't so unusual. People created false identities online for all kinds of reasons, many of them innocuous.

Unless Marcus Dartnell was his real name, and Spencer Jennings the made-up one? It could be that way around, couldn't it? Emily really hoped it wasn't so. The implications were far heavier than him having used a fake name on a dating site, and the potential for her friend to end up getting hurt all the greater for it.

Perhaps she should simply tell Laura what she'd found and let her decide what, if anything, to do about it. That was the sensible thing to do. This was, after all, Laura's life. It wasn't up to Emily to make decisions for her, was it?

And yet...

Again, Emily's thoughts swung back in the other direction. If what she'd seen was just a misguided effort on Spencer's part to disguise his real identity on a dating site, something he'd played around with ages ago, before he met Laura, there was no need to worry her. Not until Emily was certain what was actually going on here. But to find that out, she'd need proper information, incontrovertible facts to prove, or disprove her theory about Spencer. Quite how she was going to do that eluded her for the moment.

Emily bookmarked the page and closed the laptop. Maybe there was a way.

CHAPTER 12

Veronica stood in front of the open wardrobe and flicked through the hangers. She didn't know why she was being so uncertain; it hardly mattered what she wore. On the other hand, she didn't want to look too 'done up' – it was only the village pub – but she needed Jack to see she'd made some kind of effort.

It was almost half past seven, and she hadn't even put a comb through her hair yet. She reached for her best black trousers, hooking them off the hanger. Black trousers took you anywhere. A few minutes more, and she'd chosen a three-quarter sleeve jersey top, wine red with a tiny print, to go with them. Smart but not dressy.

Veronica changed into her outfit then sat down at the dressing table and gave her hair a good brush before coaxing it into its usual chin-length bob with the comb. She hardly wore make-up these days but she smoothed on some light foundation, then applied a pinkish-brown lipstick.

Back downstairs, Jack looked up from his paper. 'What's all this, then? Going somewhere, are you?' He stared at her with friendly curiosity, not animosity, and Veronica immediately felt guilty.

She pushed the feeling to one side. 'I said earlier, if you'd been listening. I'm popping out. I won't be long.'

'Ah yes, you did say.' Jack put his paper down on his lap. 'Didn't think you were serious. Where are you off to, exactly?'

'I told you. I'm having a drink with someone who comes in the shop. A few of them, as it goes, women I've known a while. We get on well. It was nice to be asked.'

'Oh. Well, I suppose that's all right then.' Jack's face changed a bit, his mouth turned down at the corners.

Veronica almost said she wouldn't bother going out after all. That murder thing they were following was on telly tonight. And then her mind swung back to the purpose of tonight's little mission.

'Yes, it *is* all right. I won't be late.'

She marched into the hall, wriggled into her grey jacket, swung on her shoulder bag and left the cottage.

She still felt guilty, and, if she was honest, a teeny bit nervous. She admonished herself for the feeling. What was there to be nervous about? She was a grown woman, wasn't she? More than grown. Every day she stood behind the counter, greeting every customer with a ready smile, whether she knew them or not, and she was never short of a friendly word. The shop was her own domain, it was true, but if she couldn't walk into a pub in her own village without a companion, it was a pretty poor show.

By the time she reached the Goose and Feather, all her nervousness had gone, and she pushed open the door with the confidence she'd known was in there somewhere. Veronica looked around the bar. It was so long since she'd been in here, she'd forgotten what it looked like. It was a Wednesday evening;

the pub was fuller than she'd imagined. Several pairs of eyes were on her, including those of the landlord, but she didn't mind. The faces she saw were friendly, and there were several 'hellos' as she stood a little uncertainly inside the door.

She wasn't meeting anyone, of course. She'd only told Jack she was to stop him objecting to her outing or thinking it strange, which it was, in a way. She hadn't been able to think of anywhere to take herself off to other than the Goose, and she was damned if she was going to wander around the village in the cold until she felt it was a suitable time to go home.

Maybe she should have asked someone to come with her. She had friends in the village, naturally, especially among the women who came to the shop, but none of them could be described as close enough to invite to the pub when it was such an unusual thing for her to do. So, here she was, alone, and being brave about it.

'Veronica?' A voice came from the table furthest away from the window, the darkest spot. 'Come and sit with us.'

Veronica peered through the gloom and made out the nice couple who ran the greengrocers in the high street, Nick and Anne. She went across.

'On your own, are you?' Anne said. She didn't sound shocked or surprised in the least. 'Pull up a chair. Nick, get Veronica a drink.'

'Sure.' Nick beamed at her. 'What's your poison?' He stood up, pushing his hand in his pocket.

Veronica sat down. She'd no need to worry, had she? This was her local. It was also the twenty-first century. If she fancied a drink and some company, what was to stop her?

The time raced by. Veronica sipped her second lager shandy – she'd bought the second round – and chatted happily to Nick, Anne, and quite a few other people she knew who'd come over to say hello. Nobody looked askance at her, or wondered aloud why she'd come alone. She'd had an answer ready in case they did; her husband had a cold and had gone to bed early. But maybe it was superfluous; those who knew Jack would also know he liked to keep himself to himself.

Sitting at the bar on stools were a group of men who looked like regulars. Veronica half-listened to their chat and hearty laughter while the *plock* of billiard balls and a crescendo of younger voices sounded from the back room.

'We'll be seeing you in here again, I hope,' Nick said, as Veronica rose to leave. 'We often pop in on a Wednesday.'

Anne laughed. 'We do, and not only on a Wednesday. Makes a change from looking at the same four walls.'

As she left the pub to a chorus of cheery 'goodnights', Veronica felt the guilt flow through her veins once more. It was Anne's mention of four walls that did it. She'd left Jack on his own in the evening for the first time in... she couldn't remember how long. But that was the whole point, wasn't it?

'You're not going out again, are you?' Jack said on Sunday evening, as the *Antiques Roadshow* played its opening tune. He'd laid a faint emphasis on 'again'.

Sunday was pushing it a bit, she realised. It was only four days since her last trip to the pub. But it wasn't that long until Christmas Eve; time was of the essence if she was going to succeed in her mission.

'I said I would. You don't mind, do you?' Veronica wriggled into her long coat. It was a colder night than before.

'S'pose I won't have to.' Jack gave a small sigh. Then he smiled. 'Course I don't mind. As long as you're happy, that's good enough for me.'

'Come with me if you like,' Veronica ventured, knowing full well what the answer would be. It was early days. Nothing – *nobody* – would be changing that quickly.

'No, no. I'm fine right here. I know how you women like to natter. Be careful in the dark, though, love. That pavement's getting dicey.'

'I will.' She planted a kiss on top of Jack's head, where his receding hairline met his bald patch. 'I'll only be an hour or so.'

The Goose was naturally busier than it was during the week, but she found a spot on a banquette seat, having bought herself a drink, and soon she found herself drawn into the group nearby, including two of her regular customers and the one and only male member of the book group.

The time passed pleasantly enough, and Veronica stuck to her promise and was back home in an hour and a half.

'Will you be doing it a lot, this going-out-of-a-night business?' Jack handed her a mug of hot chocolate, the last thing she wanted after a lager shandy and a large glass of white wine somebody had insisted on buying her. She thanked him anyway, aware of the slight edge to his voice.

A warning light flicked on in her head. If Jack was upset about her new activities, she couldn't let that happen. She may have started out on this route with a particular goal in mind but all she'd wanted to do was ruffle the waters a little, give him food for thought. She loved Jack just the way he was. What sort of wife would she be if it were otherwise? Party or no party, she'd have to give up her plan and accept things as they were.

But maybe not just yet. Veronica could be just as stubborn as her husband if she chose to be.

'I might go again. I'll see how I feel.' She shrugged, as if it was neither here nor there. 'It makes a change from staring at the same four walls,' she added, borrowing the words from Anne from the greengrocers.

'And from staring at the same old me.' Jack raised his eyes.

'I never said that!'

He laughed. 'I know. I'm only kiddin'. Drink your hot chocolate before it gets cold.'

CHAPTER 13

Her name was Abbey Fortune, if you could believe that. Spencer was all too familiar as to how easy it was to be misled by people's profiles on dating sites. And to mislead.

He once went out with a girl called Abbey, back in his early twenties. It hadn't ended well. She was the sister of his mate, Dan, from university; that was how they'd met. For reasons best known to himself, maybe not even that, Dan had taken his sister to the summer graduation ball and proceeded to try and offload her onto any bloke who was willing. Okay, that wasn't strictly fair. Not at the time, anyway. The girl was attractive, if a tad on the weighty side, and vivacious. She didn't need her brother's help to get off with anyone. The whole thing had become a joke, and the more they drank, Abbey included, the funnier it became.

Spencer himself had gone to the party alone. He'd found Abbey in his arms almost by accident, having been physically shoved at him by a roaring drunk Dan. Abbey had been pretty much out of it too. Lagging a little behind in the alcohol stakes, Spencer had virtually carried Abbey outside and kissed her thoroughly amongst the bushes. He hadn't tried anything more, not that night; he was never that unscrupulous. In fact, he'd never rushed a woman into bed. He'd realised early on that pressurising them didn't usually work in his favour. He'd been especially – endlessly – patient with Laura Engleby. He prided himself on his restraint there, even though she'd held him at arm's length, literally, for ages. Waiting until she was ready had paid off in the end, though. Oh yes.

He and Dan's sister, Abbey, had dated on and off, and one thing had led to another until Spencer had grown so used to having the undulations of her body wedged hotly against him in his narrow single bed that on the nights she wasn't there, he found it impossible to sleep.

But after a few months of casual bliss, Abbey made it clear she wanted commitment from him, something he'd avoided like the plague and he hadn't been about to change his ways. That was when it had all started to go wrong. She kept turning up at places where he'd be when they hadn't arranged to see one another. She posted silly cards and gifts through his letterbox. She took to ringing him late at night, when he suspected she was either drunk or high, possibly both, rambling on about how perfect they were for each other, if he would only give in to it.

The girl had a personality fault, that was the problem. Eventually, with one or two other girls in his sights, Spencer had faced her and told her exactly what she could do with the attention she foisted on him in several, well-chosen and less than polite words. Miraculously, she hadn't bothered him again.

And now, here he sat in the best bistro in Cliffhaven – not that there was much competition – waiting for another Abbey while he reminisced, none too fondly, about the first one.

The match on the dating site had come as a surprise; he'd forgotten he was still signed up. It was only in a bored moment during a meeting that he'd idly logged on and seen Abbey

Fortune's message. It was recent, too. Very recent. Maybe he was the one with the personality fault, he'd been thinking, as he seriously considered responding. Even as his finger hovered over the screen, he wondered what on earth he thought he was doing. He'd astonished himself by how easily he'd pushed Laura Engleby to the back of his mind. But then, he'd always been expert at compartmentalising.

Spencer, or Marcus, as he was tonight, providing he remembered, excused himself on the grounds that he was a normal, red-blooded male with an innate sense of curiosity. A man who liked to keep his options open. Anyway, it was fine because tonight was just a bit of fun. It would be his and Abbey's only date. Or, if they really clicked, he might see her a few more times, then that would be it. Spencer's ambitions as regards the spectacularly eligible Mrs Engleby must not be compromised – he wasn't that stupid.

Abbey Fortune had suggested the venue. She lived in Cliffhaven, apparently, so he couldn't argue with that. The small seaside town wasn't a million miles from Charnley Acre so there was a small element of risk of them being spotted by a busybody from the village. But it added an edge to proceedings, a pleasant little frisson. If you didn't live dangerously now and again, what was the point?

Spencer's train of thought hit the buffers as the door of the bistro opened for the umpteenth time. The other times, when he'd thought his date had arrived, it turned out not to be so, as any likely female had been either among a group or had a man trailing behind. Again, he was disappointed as a woman, looking promisingly like the picture on the dating site, entered and immediately waved towards a table where a man sat, alone. A man who wasn't Spencer. Or Marcus.

Spencer gazed out of the window at the blackened line where sea met sky and yawned behind his hand. Abbey was late by a good twenty minutes. Five, ten, even fifteen minutes, were minor aberrations. Twenty minutes was pushing it. He'd been stood up, that was becoming clear. He'd ordered a glass of Merlot when he'd arrived. The waiter had brought a small dish of nuts and olives to go with it, and two menus. Well, they wouldn't be needing those. Spencer drank some of his wine, intending to down the rest, pay up and slip out without drawing attention to himself. His rogue date with Abbey Fortune wasn't meant to be. Just as well, probably.

He'd finished his wine and was signalling to the waiter for the bill when the bistro door opened again, letting in a wash of freezing cold air. Anxious to be out of there and have done with the whole farcical episode, he looked across without much hope, and even less interest. The woman standing alone and eyeing him across the room looked a little older than the one in the photo; her hair was lighter in colour, and styled differently. Okay, so she'd used a not-quite-recent picture, or even somebody else's picture. Everyone did it; he didn't blame her for that. But her face was still familiar. Too familiar.

Emily – Laura's best friend! Thank God Abbey hadn't turned up. Fortunately, the waiter appeared with the bill. Spencer tapped his card on the little machine as, behind the waiter's back, he saw Emily weaving her way between the tables towards him. He arranged his features into a stiff smile. He'd have a little chat, tell her he'd had a business meeting and the guy had already left. Then he'd wish her a pleasant evening and be on his way. No harm done. Again, Spencer thanked his good luck at being stood up and resolved that if he ever did this again, he'd make sure he was miles away from his home turf.

'Don't go,' Emily said, offering a brittle smile, pulling out the chair opposite and lowering herself into it as Spencer made to stand up. 'I'm a touch late. Sorry about that.'

Late? What did she mean? Spencer's brain went into a

tailspin as it tried to work out what was going on. And then he remembered: his 'date' had made the reservation herself. He'd been pleased she'd offered to do that as it saved him the bother. She'd booked in the name of Jennings. He'd given the name out of habit as he'd arrived. Abbey, or rather, Emily, had known exactly whom she was meeting. Why hadn't he cottoned on before that this was a set-up?

Another thought was kindled and caught fire. Was this Laura's doing? Had she and Emily cooked up this little scheme between them? The back of his neck was hot, his palms felt suddenly clammy. He decided to brazen it out, make out he had no idea what she was talking about. Emily, meanwhile, was looking at him expectantly, her hands steepled in front of her mouth.

He chuckled, widened his smile. He even included a little wink, pretending he thought this was some sort of joke. 'I'm sure you're not that late for whoever you're meeting, Emily. If he hasn't waited, he doesn't deserve you. Normally, I'd be happy to entertain you but I've got somewhere to be.' He stood up, glancing futilely at his wrist where his watch would be, if he'd put it on.

Her face changed. 'Sit down, Spencer. Oops, sorry. *Marcus*.'

He sat. She gave him no choice. He felt the gaze of the waiter upon him, as well as the couple at the next table. Well, he'd be out of here in a minute, if he had anything to do with it.

It was no use pretending any longer. 'Look, Emily. I don't know what you thought you'd achieve by doing... this. One thing I do know, nothing good can come of it. Nothing good at all. Think about it. And now I'm leaving and I suggest you do the same.'

He intended to stand up but he suddenly felt a heaviness in his legs and lower body. He stayed in his seat. His heart raced. He felt shaken, and his weakness made him angry. He wasn't used to having this kind of reaction. He was the one in control, always.

Emily smiled, and tucked her hair behind one ear. 'I'm going nowhere, and neither are you. Not just yet.'

Even as she'd walked up the steps to the door of the bistro, she hadn't known if she could go through with this or not. He might not even be here; maybe the whole thing had been a stupid, terrible mistake and Spencer, or Marcus, whichever he really was, wasn't waiting to wine and dine somebody called Abbey Fortune he'd picked up online. Somebody who just happened to look like Emily's younger sister, if he did but know it.

She'd spotted him straight away, sitting alone at a table for two by the window. Immediately, Laura had sprung to her mind. Lovely, loyal, incredible Laura, who'd already suffered enough sadness in her life and didn't deserve to have her heart broken again. Because that, surely, would be the outcome. Laura was in love with Spencer, and however this ended, she wouldn't be able to forget the man in a hurry, nor the emotions he'd conjured, however badly he'd betrayed her.

Emily reminded herself why she was here: to gather evidence, irrefutable proof that Spencer was not who he said he was, before she presented that truth to Laura, as she knew she had to. She'd taken a deep breath and set off towards him.

Spencer was one second from getting up and walking out, she could tell. Once he was outside, he'd have the advantage over her, be gone before she knew it, and she hadn't finished with him yet. She hadn't even begun. But still he sat, his hands palms down on the table as if he'd been about to lever himself up.

'I might as well have a drink while I'm here,' Emily said,

feigning a confidence she didn't feel. She hailed the waiter and ordered a gin and tonic, ice, no lemon. She was driving, but one little drink wouldn't hurt. Anyway, she needed it.

Spencer poured himself a glass of water from the jug on the table.

'Look, Emily...'

'No, Spencer. *You* look...' The waiter arrived with her drink. He had two menus tucked under his arm and looked at Spencer for a clue. Spencer gave a tiny shake of his head and the waiter walked away, still carrying the menus. 'Laura is my friend. In case you were wondering, she doesn't know you've been dating other women online, because I haven't told her. Unlike you, I care about Laura. I don't want her to get hurt...'

'Neither do I, Emily,' Spencer said, a shade loudly. 'It's the last thing I want. Okay, I hold up my hands to tonight. An aberration, that's all it was. A moment of madness. I've never dated anyone else while I've been with Laura. *Never*. That was a dirty trick you played. I hope you're getting some satisfaction out of it because I'm certainly not.'

Emily almost laughed. Spencer looked affronted at her accusation. Like it couldn't possibly be true because he wasn't that sort of man.

'You say you've never two-timed Laura, and yet here you are. Honestly, what kind of fool do you think I am, Spencer? Which brings me to my next point. What's with the fake ID? I'm guessing you *are* Marcus Dartnell. Am I right?'

One look at his face told Emily she was.

'It means nothing. It's not a fake identity, it's just a name change, for business purposes. You wouldn't understand.'

'Try me. No, actually, don't. It'd be a lot of old eyewash anyway. I don't believe a word that comes out your mouth, and neither will Laura, very soon.'

Spencer's previously rigid expression became suddenly

animated. 'Please don't do that. You said yourself you don't want Laura to get hurt. She and I, well, she's come to mean a lot to me, an awful lot. I can be an idiot at times. So, I'm not perfect. Is anybody? But I promise you nothing like this will ever happen again.' Emily opened her mouth to speak but Spencer held a palm towards her, silencing her with a belligerent look. 'I don't have to explain myself to you but if you must know, I'd already realised this was a mistake. I was about to leave without seeing Abbey. *You*, I mean. I would never have gone through with it, and that's the truth.' Spencer rubbed a hand across his head. '*God...*'

However bad this was for Laura, Emily couldn't help feeling a bit triumphant that she'd managed to provoke Spencer. He was looking more uncomfortable by the minute.

It didn't last, of course it didn't. The man was too arrogant, too full of his own sense of worth, to be overly bothered about the trick she'd played on him. Scraping his chair back, he got up and headed smartly for the door. Emily rifled in her bag and left enough money on the table to cover the cost of her drink, then hurried after him. By the time she caught up with Spencer he was standing on the forecourt of the bistro, looking up and down the seafront road, presumably for a taxi, his composure back in place.

He turned to Emily. 'Are you going to blab to Laura, or not?' He shot the question at her.

'You'll just have to wait and see, won't you?'

Emily turned on her heel and headed for her car. If Spencer – *Marcus* – thought she was going to offer him a ride back to Charnley Acre, he could think again.

CHAPTER 14

Clayton's strategy to think about anything except Christmas had failed miserably so far. He wasn't thinking about Christmas itself, not the coming one, anyway; he was thinking about Louise and that tragic Christmas Eve – which amounted to the same thing, of course. And by association, his mind was also on Spencer, and moving on one step further, Laura Engleby. This inability to distract himself, he realised – too late – was the direct result of setting up camp on Laura's property, where the man himself was likely to pitch up at any moment.

Clayton wondered how long he could go on pretending there was nothing amiss while he was in Laura's presence. He'd only managed to stop himself from blurting out Spencer's guilty secret by reminding himself of how hurt she'd be to find out from a third party – a heavily involved third party, at that. She might turn on Clayton and accuse him of trying to wreck her relationship. He wouldn't blame her if she did; under those circumstances, refusal to accept the truth would be a normal reaction, and Laura turning against him was the last thing he wanted – he understood enough about his own feelings, complicated though they were, to know that. In fact, he missed Laura, quite acutely, when she wasn't around. Like now.

It was Friday, the fourth day of the Christmas tree sales. Business had been slow to begin with, but it was picking up nicely now. They'd sold four trees already this morning, and it was only half past ten. The pattern had been the same when they'd had the pitch in the village. The eager ones were there like a shot to get the pick of the trees, having noted the date from the posters around the village or the ad in the *Cliffhaven News*. Then, once word got round, there'd be a steady flow of customers. Some came just to stand around and chat, and treat themselves to a bag of hot chestnuts from the little brazier while they inspected the trees. Then they'd return in a day or so to make their final choice and carry away their tree. That was fine by him. Despite this being all about Christmas, it was a social occasion, too. Clayton had trained himself to enjoy that aspect of the tree sales, and shut out everything else. Well, he'd just have to try harder to do that this year.

He hadn't seen much of Laura lately. By the time he and Saul arrived at around half past nine, she'd already left for work, and it got dark so early now that they tended to pack up around four, before she was back. But she'd come home early on Wednesday, and Clayton had been pleased beyond reason to see her car turn in at the gates at around half three. She'd tooted as she'd passed up the drive, and he'd felt a pinch of disappointment that she hadn't stopped. Then, not long afterwards, as he'd released a tree from the netting machine for a customer, he'd looked up to find her standing uncertainly to one side, as if she was concerned about getting in the way. As if she need worry about that.

Until then, he hadn't seen her to speak to since they'd had coffee in the Ginger Cat, more than a week and a half ago – despite his best-laid plans, he'd missed her when he'd come to give her garden its winter trim. She hadn't stopped long, just long enough to ask how they were getting on and was there anything they needed. He'd wished he could have thought of something, or at least found some reason to keep her there, but by the time he'd taken the money for the netted tree, she was already walking back towards the house.

'Clayton?'

He turned, realising this was the second time Saul had spoken. He peeled his eyes away from the entrance, where he'd been keeping a pointless watch for Laura's car.

'This lady wants a six-foot Fraser fir and she hasn't got a roof-rack. Can we deliver?'

'Of course, no problem.' Clayton smiled at the petite, smartly-dressed woman.

'I always do this,' she said, smiling back apologetically. 'I come intending to get a little one but then I get carried away. These have such a gorgeous, citrussy scent, just like all the fruits of Christmas, don't you think?'

'Definitely. Those are my favourites too,' Clayton lied.

As the customer for the Fraser fir teetered back to her car in her high-heeled suede boots, the track on the portable CD player switched to Bing Crosby singing 'White Christmas'. Clayton groaned, and tugged his beanie hat further down over his ears.

'Told you this one was dire last year,' Saul said. 'I'll bring some decent music tomorrow, shall I? I've got some old CDs kicking about somewhere.'

'No thanks. I've heard your idea of decent music and it won't be Christmassy, that I do know.'

Saul chuckled. 'Put the carols back on, then, shall I?'

Christmas carols were even more depressing; most of them were dirges. Clayton felt a pall of gloom descend on him, as dark and heavy as the skies above the distant hills. It seemed harder than ever this year to keep his mood from plummeting. In silent answer to his assistant, he pushed his way past the forest of branches, ducked beneath the tarpaulin they'd erected as a shelter and switched the CD player off altogether.

Laura and her fellow teachers had cut short this afternoon's pageant rehearsal. It was the first time all the children from the various classes had got together in an attempt to inject some cohesion into the pageant. Unfortunately, there'd been a fire drill this morning, and the more excitable kids were still on a high from the unscheduled exit.

Then, just as Laura had managed to line up Red Class, remind the doubtful ones whether they were kings, donkeys, lambs or angels, and showed them how to walk correctly across the stage, a boy from Blue Class had spotted a few flakes of snow fluttering past the floor-to-ceiling windows of the hall, and shouted out about it. The almost orderly procession had immediately broken apart and scattered, like beads from a snapped necklace. Naturally, by the time the kids had raced to the windows, there was no further sign of snow.

'I bloody well give up,' Jeff, Blue Class's teacher, had hissed in Laura's ear. 'All they have to do is the same as they did last year.'

They'd laughed then, because if you didn't laugh you'd do the other thing. It wasn't the children's fault, of course, and on the day, the pageant would go off swimmingly, as it always did. The mistakes and toppling scenery would all add to the atmosphere, tantrums would be swept aside and the parents, as well as the kids, would be proud and tearfully happy.

Laura couldn't help feeling grateful that today's rehearsal had descended into chaos, though. She'd been looking forward all day to going home again, and now she had the bonus of being able to leave on time. The Christmas trees at the bottom of her garden had looked so pretty this morning, propped up within the metal stands: homely, wide-based triangles of Nordmann firs touching green fingers with bushy Norway spruces; distinctive blue-green Noble firs and elegant Frasers forming forests of their own among the glossy-leaved rhododendron bushes.

Having all this valuable merchandise on her property had been quite a worry at first, and Laura had expressed her concerns to Clayton. He'd assured her he'd never had a tree stolen yet, and the chains he fixed around the trees left on the plot would be sufficient. Laura couldn't help thinking his attitude was a bit laid-back, but that, as she was rapidly learning, was typical Clayton. Well, it certainly beat Spencer's habit of homing in on every tiny thing that could possibly go wrong.

And there she went again, comparing Spencer and Clayton. It was unfair of her.

'*Stop it*,' she admonished herself, as she came off the motorway and took the road to Charnley Acre.

Then she laughed. Sure, she was looking forward to seeing the trees, and hearing the carols playing, and eating the hot chestnut Saul would drop into her hand, laughing as she flinched against the heat. But more, she was looking forward to seeing Clayton. The connection between them was unmistakable; it wasn't her imagination playing tricks. She'd noticed it most strongly when they'd sat opposite one another in the Ginger Cat. His attention had been focussed on her so completely that it had turned the occasion into something much more intimate than simply having coffee with a friend.

What all this meant she had yet to work out. Nothing, probably. Well, nothing more than a silly crush on her part and a spot of lust on Clayton's. It couldn't mean anything deeper, because she was with Spencer, and Clayton knew it. He didn't strike Laura as the relationship-wrecker type. Not that it would ever go that far. She may be unwittingly encouraging Clayton – if he could read her mind then she definitely was – but if she couldn't control her impulses at her age, it was a pretty poor show. There was no reason to rush home, then. No reason at all.

Laura glanced at the clock on the dashboard and put her foot down.

'Hey, you caught us,' Clayton said, smiling as Laura walked towards him, having quickly parked her car.

'Why, what were you up to?'

'Now, that would be telling.' He tapped the side of his nose.

She and Clayton both laughed. Saul just raised his eyes.

An elderly couple had pulled up in their equally elderly Morris Minor Traveller and were making their way back down the drive. Clayton, ever the friendly businessman, stepped smartly forward to greet them.

'What happened to the music?' Laura said to Saul, as she nipped across the boards to where the CD player sat silently on the ground. 'Have the batteries died? Let me have a look. I might have some indoors that will fit.'

Saul glanced towards Clayton, who was lifting the couple's choice of tree to the ground so that they could inspect it. 'It was doing his head in. He turned it off ages ago.'

Laura frowned. 'It's not very Christmassy, is it? When you were down in the village, didn't you have fairy lights strung about, and some of those snowmen with the wobbly heads?' She'd just realised why the sales plot looked a bit bare this year, and it wasn't only because of the new location.

'We did,' Saul said. 'They're all in the van, as it goes. I keep saying when are we getting it sorted but he keeps putting it off.'

'Clayton?'

'Yep.' Saul looked at Laura as if she was stupid. She was surprised, that was all.

Saul looked Clayton's way before he spoke again, as if to check that he wasn't listening, but he was deep in conversation with the couple about how to prevent needle-drop.

'He doesn't do Christmas. I reckon that's why he hasn't put all the trappings out. Because we're up here he thinks we can do without.'

'Doesn't do Christmas?' Again Laura felt she must have an idiotic look on her face. 'You mean Clayton doesn't *like* Christmas?'

Who didn't like Christmas? What was there about it *not* to like? Laura stared after Clayton, who was trudging up the drive now, carrying the elderly couple's tree to their car while they trotted behind.

'His sister was killed on Christmas Eve,' Saul said. 'It was about five years ago now.'

'Oh my God.' Laura clapped hand to her mouth. 'What happened?'

'Louise was mown down by a hit-and run-driver on her way home from a party. She was living with Clayton at the time. The bastard got away with it, too. I remember Mum and Dad talking about it at the time. Clayton lodged with us before he bought Mistletoe Cottage. That's how we knew him.'

For a moment, shock took away Laura's power of speech. How the hell did somebody get away with a hit-and-run?

Saul read her mind. 'The bloke who did it claimed he thought he might have knocked down a deer. Reckoned he had no idea it was a person. He only went back later because he thought he should do something about it. By the time he'd found her and called the ambulance it was too late.'

'And the police didn't question his story?' Laura was incredulous.

'Oh yes, they questioned it, but she'd had a couple of drinks and could have been wandering about in the middle of the road for all anyone knew. He hadn't been drinking, or if he had it had worked its way through. Dark night, no witnesses, the best lawyer money could buy, and job done.'

'They let him off *completely*?'

'Did him for careless driving. He got a fine and a ban. Clayton nearly got done for contempt of court. He let him have what for from the public gallery.' A swift smile crossed Saul's face. 'He knew his sister would've been careful walking home. She'd phoned him before she left the party and she wasn't even kaylied.'

Laura was silent, imagining the courtroom scene, and Clayton being reprimanded for speaking out.

'Poor Clayton,' she said, half to herself. 'He must have been desperate.'

'Yep. He spoke to a lawyer afterwards but he said that unless there was any new evidence, the police wouldn't reopen the case, and he'd have to let it go...'

Clayton returned. Laura stepped away from Saul, feeling guilty for talking about him behind his back. She was glad Saul had told her, while at the same time she wondered why he had.

Clayton gave her such a warm smile that she had to turn away to hide the tears that were forming.

'Do you want to choose yours?' he said, thinking she was inspecting the trees. 'I could take it up to the house before we pack up, if you like.'

Laura swallowed, turned round and found a smile. 'Thanks,

but I'll leave it till another day.' All she could think of right now was that poor girl, and Clayton's sadness.

Laura's heart was heavy as she walked back up to the house a few minutes later. Even if that driver had thought he'd knocked over a deer, he should have stopped straight away. What sort of a man left an animal to suffer? But it hadn't been an animal, had it? If Clayton was certain the driver was lying, then she believed it too, the same as Saul obviously did.

Reaching her doorstep, Laura had to fight off the urge to run back down and gather Clayton into a hug. She couldn't bear to think of him being so unhappy at Christmastime, or at any time. That afternoon, when he'd called unexpectedly while she was sorting the boxes of decorations... she'd seen something then, a sadness in his expression that had lasted no more than a few seconds. It had made her wonder, but she hadn't known him well enough to question it.

Nor did she now, Laura reminded herself, going in and closing the front door after her. She mustn't ever mention what happened; it wasn't as if she could offer him any comfort. It was five years ago, Saul had said. It would have been in the papers at the time, and talked about in the village. She couldn't remember anything about it, but perhaps that wasn't so surprising. That Christmas, James had been in the last stages of his life. He'd been allowed home from hospital and had lain in his bed, hooked up to a morphine pump, a nurse from the hospice close at hand. All Laura's concerns had been for him and Holly. The rest of the world had melted away.

Laura felt a rush of sadness on her own account. She went through to the living room, picked up Cynthia from beside the sewing box and clutched her tightly, holding the little doll close to her heart. After that dreadful year, Laura might have hated every Christmas from then on, the same as Clayton did. It could so easily have gone that way. But she knew James wouldn't have wanted her to live like that. Besides, there was Holly to consider; her daughter's Christmases must be filled with light and sparkle and magic, not sadness and painful memories.

Holding Cynthia up in front of her, Laura smiled into the fixed, blue eyes of the tatty old fairy doll, resplendent in her new pink costume. Christmas was a time of joy, a time of loving and forgiving. But she would never, ever forgive the man who had snatched Clayton's sister away.

CHAPTER 15

Saul jumped down from the van near the bus stop, raised a hand at Clayton as he drove away, and began to walk the short distance along the road to home.

He shouldn't have told Laura about Clayton's sister and the hit-and-run. Yes, he'd made a mistake there. As soon as he saw her face, he'd realised he should have kept his big mouth shut. They were friendly, those two. More than that, they fancied each other rotten; their body language couldn't be more telling if it tried.

They never missed a chance to get together, either; Saul had noticed that. If they were working on the garden at Spindlewood and Laura was about, the chances of Clayton accepting tea in her kitchen were sky high, even though he might have been quaffing the stuff from a flask all morning. Today was another example. As soon as Laura had got home from work, she'd hardly had time to park the car before she'd come hot-footing it back down the drive, the same as she'd done the other day. It wasn't as if she'd had any particular purpose, except perhaps to keep an eye on what was happening to her garden. It wasn't that, of course. She'd wanted to see Clayton, pure and simple, and he, in turn, was as pleased to see her as a dog with two tails.

So, Saul thought, as he reached home and cut across the garden to enter by the kitchen door, what would happen next? If the two of them were as close as he imagined, would Laura offer her sympathies to Clayton over his sister's death, and would Clayton be dead pissed off that Saul had gone and blabbed to her? That could make things a tad awkward between him and Clayton. More than a tad, if Clayton decided he wasn't to be trusted. Well, there was nothing he could do about it now. That ship had well and truly sailed, so it was pointless worrying anymore.

Saul grabbed a fruit scone from the cooling rack on the kitchen island as he passed, walloped on a lump of butter from the dish and took a large bite. It was deliciously warm and crumbly. There was no sign of his mum, but the telly was on in the den, so she was probably in there with Katy, watching one of Katy's dumb American teen dramas. He'd catch up with them in a bit. Meanwhile, he had important business to attend to.

Reaching his room, Saul dropped onto the bed, undid the laces of his work boots and kicked them off. He was supposed to take them off by the back door, but usually he forgot. They weren't all that muddy anyway, since he'd only been selling Christmas trees, not doing any actual gardening. Taking his mobile from his pocket, he checked for messages – not for the first time today. Nothing. Well, there was one from George and another of his mates but nothing from Holly Engleby.

He didn't need to check when he'd last heard from her; it was one week and one day ago – one week and half a day, to be precise. He'd sent her a text, a casual *How's it going?* kind of thing. Three days later, when he was on the point of giving up hope of a reply, her text had pinged through. *Hiya. I'm good, thanks. Working hard, hope you are too. Right now in lunch queue. Talk to you later.* She'd added a smiley.

Three days, though. He wondered why she'd waited so long to reply, but she must be dead busy, with it being near the end of term and everything. The *talk to you later* thing wasn't meant to be taken literally; it was just one of those throwaway phrases. God, if she had actually rung him, he'd have been over the bloody moon and back! He'd had a wild idea about ringing her instead of texting, but decided it would seem too much like chasing. Nobody liked to look desperate, least of all himself. No, best to keep it cool and be patient.

But not that patient. According to her mother, Holly wouldn't be home for another week at least; a gentle little reminder that he'd be here, waiting to see her, wouldn't hurt, would it?

Saul thought for a few moments, then pressed in a text: *Hi, I just realised you'll be home soon. Looking forward to seeing you. Will buy you first drink in the Goose. x*

The kiss sign might have been a bit girly and OTT. But hey, he'd sent it now, and it wasn't that inappropriate, remembering that night, back in October; a night he couldn't wait to repeat. He hoped Holly couldn't, either.

Saul slid the phone into his jeans pocket and lay back on the bed for a nice little daydream about Holly, and the pleasures in store.

It was ten o'clock on Saturday morning. Still in her pyjamas, Holly sat cross-legged on top of her bed, yanked the laptop towards her and propped it up on the leopard-print cushion that one of her housemates had given her as a joke. As she opened the laptop, the rough draft of her essay on the romantic poets popped up, rough being a generous description. The essay had been due in at four o'clock yesterday, but she'd managed to blag an extension until Monday because she'd had a throat infection. The illness was genuine – the doctor's note said so – but it hadn't stopped her seeing Lorcan last night. Nothing short of the Black Death could have stopped her doing that.

At least she hadn't been drinking. The antibiotics had put paid to that, which meant she had a clearish head this morning. In fact, she felt a lot better altogether. Her eyes strayed from the screen to the view from the window. It wasn't an exciting view, just the other side of the Birmingham street with big old terraced houses similar to this one, many of them divided up into student accommodation. But she wasn't really looking at the view. Instead she saw Lorcan, with his chocolatey-brown hair all messed up where she'd run her hands through it, the smile that made his face shine, and his compact, huggable body. He hadn't stayed the night – they hadn't done anything like that yet – but the way things were going, it wouldn't be long.

Holly hadn't intended to fall in love in her first term, but fate had other ideas, and besides, he was so damned *cute* that she hadn't been able to help herself. He'd invited her to a Halloween party at his student house, which was where it had all begun. It wasn't a forever kind of love; she was too much of a realist to believe that, as was Lorcan. They were too young to think of making a lifetime commitment, they'd both agreed on that.

But still, you never knew how life was going to pan out. She thought of her mum. Losing her dad had been the saddest, most tragic thing ever, and it always would be. At the time, the idea of her mother being with somebody else had never entered Holly's head. When her mum met Spencer, she'd been careful to explain to Holly that she could never love anyone as much as she'd loved Dad but she didn't want to be on her own forever more. She'd been trying to spare Holly's feelings, obviously, because how did Mum know she wouldn't love another man as much as she'd loved Dad? Well, she didn't know, that was the truth of it, and Holly was fine with that. All she wanted was for her mum to be happy. But with Spencer Jennings? *Really*?

He was quite good-looking, if you liked that sort of romance-novel tall-dark-and-handsome look, which Holly didn't, and she didn't think Mum did either. Spencer was too smooth, like he'd been sandpapered down. There was nothing quirky or mysterious or... *interesting* about him. The plain fact was, Spencer was okay, and that was all you could say about him. The relationship had lasted, though, which made Holly think she might have missed something, and perhaps when she got home and saw Spencer again, she'd realise there was a whole lot more to him than she'd thought.

And that, Holly said to herself, was about as likely as her getting anything more than a lower B for this essay. She looked back at the words on the screen, then at the three textbooks and pile of lecture notes on the desk, and felt totally uninspired. It might help if she got showered and dressed. Despite the heat from the radiator, which had developed an annoying tapping noise, it was chilly in here. There'd been a thick frost first thing; she'd noticed that when she'd gone down to the kitchen earlier to make tea and toast.

Thinking about frost and wintry weather reminded her of home. The garden looked so pretty and delicate with a sparkling of white, as did the woods and fields around Charnley Acre. Really Christmassy. *Christmas*. She couldn't wait. What was it Mum had been going on about when she'd rung the other night? Something about Christmas trees being sold in their garden? She hadn't been paying full attention because she'd had to leave Lorcan in the pub while she'd gone outside to take the call. It was all to do with Green and Fragrant, those people who did the gardening at Spindlewood. Holly bit her lower lip as her mind belatedly made the connection. There were only the two gardeners. One was Clayton, the owner of the business, whom Holly couldn't help but notice was pretty hot, despite being as old as the hills – or at least as old as Mum. The other was Saul. If she'd got this right, she'd be practically falling over him every time she came out of the front door.

She hadn't replied to his text yet, the one he'd sent yesterday. She felt a bit guilty about that, but the truth was she didn't know how to respond. Saul was great; she liked him a lot. He was good-looking too; black hair and blue eyes were one of her favourite combinations in a bloke. She'd known him as one of the village crowd since she was a kid, but it wasn't until the October reading week that she'd begun to see him in a different light. With a couple of drinks inside her, it had been easy to get carried away, and she'd encouraged him far more than she should have done because she was having such a good time.

She'd noticed the way Saul's mates had ribbed him for making a beeline for her as soon as she walked into the pub. The girls had done the same with her, but they'd both laughed it off. The old village grapevine had done its work, too, because her mum had mentioned Saul to Holly, pretending to be dead casual about it when really she wanted to know what was going on between them. Naturally, Holly hadn't given anything away – not that there was much to give.

If she had to describe how it was with Saul, she'd say it was like a holiday romance, only in reverse. And this was where she had to be *really* careful because, reading what lay behind Saul's texts, he was expecting to carry it on over the Christmas holidays, and that was never going to happen. She may not be with Lorcan forever, but they were together for now, and they weren't seeing anyone else meanwhile. Besides, it would be so unfair on Saul. Getting with him for a bit of fun at Christmas would be like using him, and she'd never do that.

Holly jumped off the bed, toppling the laptop. Grabbing a towel from the radiator, she padded along to the bathroom and took a shower. Back in her room, she was wriggling into her jeans when her phone lit up with a new message. She hoped it wasn't Saul again. Holding her breath, she viewed the message. A giggle escaped as Lorcan's name appeared. *Morning gorgeous, fancy doing something this afternoon?* They'd already arranged to meet tonight. It was so sweet of Lorcan, and typical, that he couldn't wait till then. Holly righted the laptop on its cushion and stared at the pathetic beginnings of her essay. She could smash it, if she put the work in this morning. She texted back, and got a happy smiley in return.

Okay, she might as well reply to Saul now, before she started work, and get that out of the way. She brought up his text and pressed in a reply. *Yep, not long till Christmas. I'm sure I'll be in the Goose at some point. Catch you then.* Friendly, but vague. No smiley, and no reciprocal *x*. Definitely not.

Throwing the phone onto the bed, Holly pulled on a pair of thick socks and a sweater and went out of the room. Ten minutes later, she was back with a mug of hot chocolate and a toasted buttered muffin. She moved the laptop to the desk by the window and sat down. The sooner she started work, the sooner she'd be free to indulge in the pleasures of the day.

CHAPTER 16

Laura hung the dress she'd chosen to wear tonight on the front of the wardrobe before leaving her bedroom, crossing the landing and taking the short flight of stairs to the turret room. Gazing out of the window, she could see the tops of the Christmas trees that had been left *in situ* overnight, and the sagging roof of the tarpaulin. The site, masked in shadow by the fading day, looked bereft without its human element. Without Clayton.

Today, Saturday, had been busy. Cars had been up and down the drive all day. She'd gone outside to chat to some of her friends from the village as she'd spotted them arriving but had stayed away from the tree site in case she betrayed her emotions. Since Saul's revelation yesterday, she hadn't been able to stop thinking about Clayton.

What did not 'doing' Christmas, as Saul had put it, actually mean? She hoped it didn't mean he would spend the day entirely alone. No matter how down he felt, that couldn't be good for him. Did he have parents or siblings to be with, family members who had shared the tragic loss of Louise? She tried to remember if he'd ever mentioned them in conversation, but nothing came to mind. Questions burned themselves into her brain; questions she had no right to express. Best, then, to keep her distance from Clayton.

She'd spent most of the day in the dining room, where she could keep a watch on what was going on outside. There she'd unpacked several parcels which had arrived during the week, including one containing three new scented candles in glass jars. She'd already lit one of the candles, standing the jar on the dining-room windowsill. The scent, a delicious mixture of sugar and spice, permeated the hallway and floated up the stairs. Other parcels had contained a string of pink fairy lights shaped like ballet shoes which she hadn't been able to resist, although she wasn't exactly short of lights. Then there were little presents to go on the tree for the family party on Christmas Day, including snowman motif socks for Holly and Laura's sister, and glittery make-up purses for her young teenage nieces.

The Christmas cards were written and waited in piles, one for posting, one for handing out personally, and some of the larger presents were wrapped and labelled. In less than a week, if she was as good as her word, Holly would be home. Laura's insides skittered with excitement at the thought. She must make sure the decorations were up by then, including the tree which she hadn't yet chosen from Clayton's stock. She wouldn't be able to avoid him altogether, then. Laura sighed, but she couldn't help the smile that crept to her lips.

The landline phone began to ring. Leaving the turret room, she hurried back down to her bedroom, reaching the extension phone just before the answer machine kicked in.

'Only me,' Emily said. 'I was just wondering what you were up to.'

Laura glanced at the silky, midnight-blue dress hanging on the wardrobe and sighed again. 'I've got to go to some function with Spencer. A dinner dance.'

'*Dinner dance*?' Emily sounded incredulous. 'Do they really still have those? I thought they went out in the eighties, if not before.'

'I wish.'

Laura's body felt suddenly heavy. She went across and sank onto the window seat. To think, she used to love swanning into luxurious country hotels, like the one they were going to tonight, on Spencer's arm, and sipping a champagne cocktail while he introduced her to his business pals and their partners. It was the novelty, she supposed. Now, though... well, she wasn't looking forward to tonight one bit.

'You don't have to go if you don't want to,' Emily said. 'Make some excuse. Not that you should need one.'

'It's not that simple.'

'Laura, it *is* that simple. What happened to your independent spirit, girl?'

'Still intact, but I don't want to let Spencer down.'

Laura frowned. This conversation had a slightly odd feel to it. Emily had always been the cheerleader in her relationship; she'd obviously thought it was high time it moved up a gear. So why was she now encouraging Laura to bow out of a date just because she didn't fancy it?

'Tell him you're ill. That'll keep him at bay.'

Laura laughed. Spencer had a horror of catching germs. Once when she'd had a cold he'd stayed away from her for ten whole days.

'I can't do that,' she said, still laughing. 'Anyway, it might not be so bad. The food will be delicious, the wine will flow, and I've got to know some of the people who'll be there. They're all quite friendly. Yes, it'll be fine.'

'Who are you trying to convince?' Emily asked, her voice quietening.

'Em, what *is* this?' Laura said.

A small silence fell before Emily spoke again. 'Nothing, take no notice of me. Get dressed up and enjoy the night. Give Spencer a kiss from me. Oh, no, forget I said that. He ain't my type.'

They both giggled. Laura felt better about tonight already, as if she really had convinced herself she wouldn't be bored rigid. If you loved somebody, though, you had to make the odd sacrifice.

'Come to lunch tomorrow, Em. Bring Wilf and we can take him for a long walk in the afternoon. It'll do us good. Well, me really. I don't get nearly enough exercise.'

'Ah, well, that's what I'm ringing about, apart from seeing how you are.'

'What, exercising?'

'No, I'm ringing about Wilf. I haven't had the chance to tell you but I met this guy on a dating site. He's in television and he works in London but he lives in Sussex...'

Emily didn't need to say any more. Laura smiled into the room.

'You've got a hot date and you want me to have Wilf? Of course I will. That means it'll be a late one then?'

It wasn't really a question. Laura would have nudged Emily in the ribs if she'd been there in person.

'I don't know. It depends. Best to be prepared, though. We went out on Thursday night and really hit it off. He's in London again this weekend but he'll be back tomorrow afternoon. I'm driving up to his and no doubt we'll have a drink, so...'

So she wouldn't be able to drive home. And the rest.

'Em, it's fine. You don't have to explain. I'll have Wilf overnight and pop him back to yours on my way to work on Monday.'

Laura heard Emily's long exhalation of breath at the other end of the line. 'Thanks. I need a bit of fun. It's been bloody *ages*.'

Laura laughed, knowing exactly what kind of fun Emily had in mind. 'Ring me tomorrow when you're on the way with Wilf. And don't forget to bring his bed and his dinner.'

'Cheers, you're a darling,' Emily said, and rang off.

Laura stayed sitting on the window seat for a moment, thinking about Emily and her exciting, but brave, dating activities. She did hope this one worked out for her. It was a lottery wasn't it, dating virtually strange men? How were you supposed to know they were genuine? It was different with her and Spencer. She'd got to know him fairly well before she'd spent time at his house, or let him come to hers. And as for sleeping with him, she'd made him wait ages, well past the point of sense. To his credit, he'd seemed perfectly happy to wait until she was ready, and hadn't put any pressure on her.

When you'd had one partner for years, starting all over again was a nerve-wracking experience. But eventually, she'd learned to trust her own judgement, and now here she was again, preparing to play the part of Spencer's partner in public.

Play the part. Where had that come from? She *was* Spencer's partner, so why did she feel as if she was stepping into a role when she was out with him, a role she no longer seemed to fit?

It was a quarter to four on Sunday afternoon when, having waved off a sparkly-eyed Emily, Laura took Wilf for his walk. The sun had shone brightly all day, but now the sky was streaked with rose and apricot as sunset approached, and the air already held a hint of the frost to come.

They walked down the drive, past the deserted Christmas tree plot, and out onto the road. Laura had planned to head up the hill, then follow the public footpath as far as the stile before turning back. But Wilf, apparently, had other ideas and trotted determinedly in the other direction, leading Laura instead of the other way around. Fine, she thought. The village it is, then. No doubt it would turn out to be a longer walk but they were both well wrapped up against the cold, Laura in her old cord jeans, padded jacket and blue woolly hat; Wilf in his red quilted coat.

As they made their way down the hill, Laura thought about last night. Apart from the seemingly endless self-congratulatory speeches made by several of the business federation's members, she'd had quite a good time. Spencer had been charming and funny; he'd even danced with her, to the slow numbers. In fact, he'd seemed to be making an extra effort to make sure she enjoyed herself.

The event had finished before midnight. He hadn't stayed over. Their goodnight kisses on her doorstep had been passionate, and she'd expected him to pay off the taxi. Unusually for Spencer, he'd seemed unsure as to what came next. In the end, he'd said he was tired and would she mind if he didn't come in. Of course she didn't mind, she'd assured him – which happened to be true – but still, she'd felt slightly puzzled as she'd watched him get back in the taxi.

While she'd been getting ready for bed she'd remembered how, during the evening, Spencer had quizzed her, quite intently, about the Christmas trees. He'd seemed concerned about the constant visitors disrupting her privacy as well as the possible damage to the garden. She'd assured him that there hadn't been any problems, nor did she expect there to be.

Lulled into a happy haze by the excellent wine, she hadn't paid too much attention at the time. Now, she wondered if all this interest was because Spencer was still angry with her over Clayton, and that was why he hadn't wanted to stay last night. She'd noticed, too, that Spencer hadn't come anywhere near Spindlewood while the trees were on sale. Well, if he wanted to sulk, that was his problem, not hers. She would ring him this evening, though, just to make sure he was okay. She shouldn't find fault with Spencer so readily, not if she really loved him.

Christmas had come to Charnley Acre, or at least the beginnings of it, Laura was happy to note, as she and Wilf passed a row of five timbered cottages that were some of the oldest in the village. Two had holly wreaths on the low-lintelled doors, and lighted trees in the windows. Through the window of another, she glimpsed a ceiling-high swoop of sparkle. Some of the shops in the high street already had festive window displays. The Ginger Cat's inside windowsill had disappeared under a froth of fake greenery, and strings of cardboard cats wearing party hats and unlikely grins were looped across the window itself. Veronica's wool and craft shop had huge red and green bows attached to the baskets of wool in the window. Even the hardware shop had sprigs of fake holly between the mops and buckets and pots of paint, and reindeer stickers on the window.

The Christmas market would begin in a few days' time. The stalls were already being set up in the car park, spilling round the corner, into the high street. There'd be fewer parking spaces in the village but only the miseries would complain, and once the stalls came to life with fairy lights, bunting, music and the usual colourful array of handmade gifts, decorations and all kinds of delicious things to eat, any ill feeling would be soon forgotten.

Laura loved it all; she smiled with satisfaction as she continued along the street. She couldn't wait to begin on her own decorations. Spindlewood was made for Christmas. The spacious, high-ceilinged hallway was the ideal place for the tree; they'd always placed it there, with Cynthia on top, presiding over the festivities. The mantelpieces above the fireplaces in the living and dining room cried out for greenery, red ribbons and fairy lights. Deep windowsills throughout the house made good homes for candles swathed with ivy, baubles piled into glass bowls, and the miniature shops and houses with lighted windows, which were Holly's favourites. She could make a start tonight, if she had the energy after her walk.

Laura wandered contentedly along, thinking about Christmas, the whippet trotting beside her. Outside the shuttered post office, Wilf stopped to use the lamp-post before taking a sharp turn down the side street, Laura following. It was growing dark now; she'd give Wilf five more minutes, then they'd make their way back to the high street, and home.

Reaching the end of Wilf's chosen street, Laura had just shortened his lead, preparing to guide him along the shortest route home, when a street name caught her eye: Squirrel Lane. Wasn't this where Clayton lived? She recalled the address from his invoices. Laura hesitated. Squirrel Lane led eventually to the main Charnley Road. It would take longer to get home that way than if they doubled back to the high street, but that was all right. A good walk now would mean Wilf would only need a quick mooch around the garden tonight.

As if that was ever going to be the reason.

Shaking her head at her own hopelessness, Laura set off along Squirrel Lane. The house wasn't difficult to spot; the bright-green van was parked alongside it. Nerves zigzagged through her as she and Wilf drew level with the row of Victorian flint cottages. Clayton's was at the far end of the row. *Mistletoe Cottage*, Laura read on the wooden sign attached to the gate. Strangely enough, as soon as she saw the sign, her nerves left her. She felt reassured, whether it was because of the lovely name of the cottage, or the fact Clayton lived there, she didn't know. Either way, there was no reason to feel guilty at being here.

Even so, she averted her eyes from the windows as Wilf enforced a stop right outside the house in order to sniff the sprouting of grass that grew by the gatepost. It wouldn't do to be caught peeking.

'Hey!' Clayton's voice came out of nowhere. 'Laura!'

She gazed round confusedly. There was nobody at the front door, nor at the window. And then Clayton was beside her, a broad grin on his face.

'Oh, hello. I didn't see...' Laura began.

'I was looking for something in the back of the van,' Clayton said, waving in the direction of the van which she could now see had its back doors open. 'I don't need to ask what you're doing along here.'

'What? Oh, yes...' Laura said, as she realised Clayton was looking down at Wilf.

A beat of silence, then she smiled. 'We've been out a while – his idea, not mine. It's time we were heading back.'

She yanked pointedly on Wilf's lead but the dog didn't budge. Instead, he transferred his sniffing activities to Clayton's shoes, then, embarrassingly, licked the hem of his jeans. Laura raised her eyes.

Clayton stooped to pat Wilf's head. 'I think he likes me.'

'He's a whippet. He likes everybody.'

'And there was I thinking I was someone special.'

Laura couldn't meet Clayton's gaze. There was something about the way he'd said that which made her think he wasn't talking about the dog. How come she was here, outside his house, anyway? Hadn't she decided to avoid Clayton, after what Saul had told her? Well, that hadn't lasted long, had it?

'Kettle's on,' Clayton said, nodding towards the cottage. 'Or it will be in a tick.'

'That's usually my line.' Laura laughed. 'Thanks, but I mustn't hold you up any further.'

He smiled. 'You wouldn't be.'

CHAPTER 17

Clayton threw tea bags into two mugs, or tried to. Both missed their target the first time. Laura's proximity in his small kitchen was having an unsettling effect on him. At least, he assumed that's what it was. Up at Spindlewood, her home territory, it was different. But having her here, in his home, was fostering the same kind of intimacy as there was that morning in the Ginger Cat. He wondered if Laura had also noticed it then and whether she was aware of it now. But when he turned round, having finally succeeded in producing two passable mugs of tea, he saw only composure. She'd taken off her hat along with her coat, and her hair was all mussed up on top. He liked that.

'Take this through, shall we? It's cosier in there.'

He led the way to the living room and invited her to sit on the sofa, in front of the log burner. Passing Laura her tea, he rustled the Sunday paper he'd been reading onto the floor and sat down at the other end of the sofa.

'Sorry, I've haven't got a coffee table. Put it on the floor when you're done.'

'Thanks,' she said, immediately curling her hands round the mug.

'It's turned cold out.'

'Yes.' She took a few sips. 'Lovely, just what I needed. I'll just have this, then we'll be out from under your feet.'

'No need. I wasn't doing much. He looks settled, anyway.' He nodded towards the dog, who'd stretched himself out on the rug in front of the fire, his head resting on his paws. 'He's not yours, is he?'

'He's Emily's. My friend. Wilf gets to hang out with me if she's going to be gone for any length of time. Or I get to hang out with him, one or t'other.'

Laura laughed; it was a little high-pitched. She wasn't quite as composed as she was making out, then. For some reason, Clayton felt pleased about that.

'I love your house,' she said, glancing about. 'It's very homely.'

'Thanks. It was a wreck when I bought it, but I think it was worth the trouble.'

'Certainly was. Like Spindlewood. I don't know how we managed to stop the whole lot collapsing in a pile of rubble, but we did. Now all I have to do is keep it upright and weatherproof, which hasn't been so easy since... Well, there you go.' She shrugged, and gave a tight little smile.

She'd been going to say, since her husband died. Clayton half-wished she had. It might have signposted the way to deeper conversations, about real, meaningful things. Things he hadn't realised he wanted to talk about, until now.

'It must take a lot of upkeep, a house of that size and age.' He turned to look at her. 'If you're ever stuck, I could do a few jobs for you. I learned one heck of a lot about DIY when I was doing up this place. Had to. Couldn't afford to get people in. Except for the replastering in the front bedroom and that had to be done by an expert if I didn't want to wake up to the Rocky Mountains every morning.'

Laura seemed a bit startled. He hadn't meant to imply that she couldn't afford to get people in either – he hoped she hadn't taken it that way. His offer was sincere, though. It would give him pleasure to help her, in any way he could, and Spindlewood was a stunner of a house. It deserved all the care and attention it could get. He doubted that Marcus – Spencer, whatever – would be getting his lily-white hands dirty any time soon. Supposing she let the man move in with her, though? She wouldn't have any worries like that then, would she? He would pay his team of tradesmen to come and sort the house out. Perhaps that's what she was thinking, too. The idea rolled a wave of depression over Clayton.

Laura was smiling now. 'Thanks, that's very kind. I'll be fine, though. I can bang the odd nail in when I have to.'

And a lot more, besides, Clayton thought. 'I'm sure you can,' he said. 'It's having the time, isn't it?'

She nodded. Her mind wasn't on the house now, he was certain of it; a faraway look had crept into those beautiful blue-grey eyes.

And then she was back in the moment, putting her mug down on the floor in a deliberate fashion, as if she'd just come to a decision. 'Clayton, who's that in the photo?'

She glanced up at the framed photo on top of the bookshelf.

'My younger sister, Louise. She died in a road accident. It'll be five years, Christmas Eve.'

Laura nodded. 'I'm so sorry.'

She seemed unsurprised. Perhaps she already knew. She wasn't about to smother him with sympathy, he could see that by her expression, and boy, was he glad about that. His mind went into overdrive before he could stop it.

Ask me how she died. No, please don't ask me how she died. Yes, ASK ME!

His heart seemed about to force its way out of his chest. Was this the moment, the moment when he shattered Laura's illusions about her boyfriend forever more? The moment he rescued her? Oh, how he wished he could be the one to do that. She was so very lovely, far too good for that man. Every minute he spent with her enhanced that.

Laura was looking at him closely, her face full of concern. 'Clayton, I'm sorry. I shouldn't have asked about the photo. I didn't mean to upset you.'

He smiled, or as near as. 'You haven't. I'm fine. Louise lived here for quite some time. She's still a part of Mistletoe Cottage and I'm glad you asked.'

He went on to tell Laura about Louise's job as a physiotherapist, how she'd moved to Sussex after their parents had both died, which had suited him, too – having his sister for company had helped take the sting out of his recent break-up. He talked about Louise's photography, and her zest for life, adding colourful little details about her, inconsequential things he hadn't thought about in a while.

As he talked about Louise's life, so the desperate need to talk about her death began slowly to recede. Laura listened quietly, her face alight with genuine interest, and again Clayton thought how strong she was, and how he could well take a leaf out of her book – the whole damn book, in fact. But whether she was strong enough to deal with the unpalatable truth about Spencer, especially if it came from him, was another matter. He didn't know her well enough to make that kind of judgement.

'Louise sounds lovely,' Laura said.

'She was.'

'This must be a difficult time of year for you.'

Clayton leaned forward, resting his forearms on his knees.

He glanced up at the photo, then down at Wilf, spread-eagled on the rug. He didn't look at Laura. 'I ignore it as far as I can. The whole Christmas thing. It's easiest to pretend it isn't happening.'

For a few moments, the only sound was the crackle of wood in the burner and the dog's soft snoring. Then Laura spoke again, her voice quiet.

'Is it easiest, though, in the long run?'

'I haven't got a clue. I haven't tried it any other way.'

Laura nodded, and gazed pensively into the fire. She might have been thinking it was time he made some changes, took a chance and see where it led him; if he had to guess what was going through her mind, that would be the favourite. But what was right for others wasn't necessarily right for him.

Laura stretched out a foot and gently nudged the dog's side. 'Come on sleepy-head. Time for home.'

Wilf opened one eye, then in one bound he was up on the sofa, oozing his long body between Clayton and Laura, and nuzzling Laura's neck.

She fondled Wilf's ear. 'Soppy old thing.'

Clayton reached out to stroke the dog's neck at the same moment that Laura's hand moved down. Their hands met, just for a moment, but long enough for Clayton to feel the warmth of Laura's fingers brushing his and the resulting electrical zing. And in that same moment, their eyes locked.

'Laura…'

But she was up, fastening the dog's lead to his harness, hurrying out of the room.

Out in the hall, she swiped her coat from the hook, shrugged into it and rammed on the woolly hat. 'Thank you for the tea.'

Clayton opened the door for her. 'See you tomorrow.'

'Tomorrow, yes.'

She was gone.

CHAPTER 18

She couldn't do this. This... whatever it was. She'd thought it was nothing more than one of life's sweet little moments, a candy-floss fantasy. Until yesterday. All through the evening, and half the night, she'd thought about little else but Clayton. He'd claimed such a huge part of her mind that she'd even forgotten to phone Spencer, as she'd intended. He hadn't phoned her either, which might mean something, or it might not; she'd given up trying to work him out. That, too, of course, was a sign that she'd wandered off track. Well, it wasn't good enough.

By the time she'd delivered Wilf back to Cloud Cottage first thing this morning, settled him down to await Emily's return, and begun the journey to school, Laura had made a new resolution – a stronger one this time – to keep her distance from Clayton Masters, as far as practically possible. When their paths did cross, she'd remind herself he was her gardener and a casual friend, and treat him accordingly. Then, hopefully, Clayton would understand, and take his cue from her. What he had made of her bolting out of his house like a frightened rabbit she couldn't imagine, but it was best not to try. The thought of him being alone at Christmas, shutting himself away in Mistletoe Cottage until it was all over, still made her sad, but that was because she cared, when really she had no right to.

As for Spencer, she'd make a much greater effort not to take his hot-and-cold moods personally. He'd told her he didn't have any work problems, but Laura wasn't sure she believed him. More than likely, he was too proud to admit to them, but there were bound to be glitches. He had a lot of responsibility with the massive projects he always seemed to have on the go. No wonder he seemed stressed out, and got irritated with her when she came out of her corner fighting all the time.

It wasn't all the time, though, was it? It was only over the Clayton thing, because, stupidly, she'd felt the need to defend him when it was Spencer she should be siding with. Why there had to be sides in the first place remained a mystery, and looked as if it would remain as such. Spencer had made it perfectly clear that any quizzing by her would be distinctly unwelcome and, frustrating though it was, she must respect that. She'd definitely ring him this evening and ask him over for dinner this week. They'd have a pleasant, relaxing evening and it would all be fine. At least, she hoped it would.

The Monday morning chaos was a welcome distraction today. Once the raggle-taggle line of children had filed into the classroom and swarmed around her, competing for her attention with their stories and endless questions, the rest of the world, necessarily, took a back seat, Spencer and Clayton included. Term would be over tomorrow and Laura was looking forward to the break. But first there was the pageant to get through, tomorrow afternoon. Some of the parents had waylaid Laura in the playground this morning with worries about costumes and timings and behaviour, and she'd reassured them that everything was under control, and all they had to do was sit in the audience and enjoy it. She'd had her fingers firmly crossed inside her pocket, of course.

A busy day, a frustrating journey home – part of the Charnley Acre road was closed due to a burst water main, meaning a detour – and Laura arrived home wanting nothing more than a cup of tea in front of the fire. She was late; Green and Fragrant would have left by now, which could only be a good thing. They hadn't. As soon as she swung into the entrance to Spindlewood there was the van in its accustomed place, and there was Clayton, attending to something under the tarpaulin. Saul was sitting in the van, his attention fixed on his phone.

Clayton's head snapped up as she approached. No chance of driving past and pretending she hadn't seen him then. She brought the car to a standstill, leaving the engine running, and let the window down as Clayton stepped up beside it.

'Hello, Laura. Do you want to come and pick your tree? I can bring it up to the house before I go then.'

'It'll be dark in a minute.'

'I think I can find my way up the drive in the dark, just about.' He smiled. Brown eyes flashed into hers.

Oh God. She wished he wouldn't do that, especially after yesterday. He must have known full well why she'd been in such a hurry to leave Mistletoe Cottage, and was choosing to ignore it. Clearly her plan to relegate Clayton to semi-formal status was doomed to failure from the start. Even so, she had to make the effort.

'That's very kind of you, Clayton, but I've got some things to do as soon as I get in. Look, why don't you pick me a tree, a nice big one, a Noble fir, maybe? Then Saul can bring it up tomorrow. If he leaves it in the porch that'll be fine.'

Clayton heeled his hands against the roof of the car. 'Laura, is everything okay?'

Well, what do you think?

'Yes, of course. Must go.'

She put the car into gear and drove off.

Resisting the urge to go up to the turret room to watch Clayton leave, Laura put a match to the ready-laid fire in the living room and sat down with her phone. Her first call was to Spencer.

He picked up in seconds. 'Hello, my lovely.'

'Gosh, you sound cheerful.'

He laughed. 'Don't I always?'

Best not to answer that, Laura thought. 'What's happening this week? Are you free for dinner at mine? I want to try out some recipes for stuff I might make for my party.'

'I'll be your guinea pig any time you like. Your cooking's tip-top.'

Laura's turn to laugh. 'Tip-top? There's an old-fashioned expression.'

She sensed Spencer's smile. 'It's a compliment. Take it or leave it.'

'I'll take it, because it happens to be true. When, then?'

'Not for a few days, I'm afraid. I've got late meetings. It's nigh on impossible to get the key people together within reasonable hours and there are decisions to be made over the village site before ruddy Christmas brings everything to a halt... never mind about that. I could do Thursday?'

Laura pushed from her mind Spencer's mention of the village site. Time to concentrate on the positives in her relationship. It was book group on Thursday – they were due to meet at Veronica's cottage in Mill Street – but she'd rather see Spencer. She hadn't read much of the book anyway. She told him Thursday was fine.

'Actually,' Spencer said, 'there is something I want to talk to you about, when I see you.'

'Oh?' Laura felt a twinge of anxiety. If Spencer was going to start on about Clayton again, she wasn't sure she could handle it.

'Don't worry, it's nothing bad. The opposite, in fact. But you'll have to wait till Thursday.'

Again, she sensed a smile as Spencer's confidence beamed across the radio waves. Strangely enough, Laura's own confidence took a dive in response. Spencer should at least have given her a clue; he knew she didn't like surprises. Or perhaps he'd forgotten that, which was equally depressing.

As the call to Spencer ended, so Emily's came through. Bang on cue, Laura thought, her darker thoughts dispelling immediately. She was smiling as she picked up the call.

'I think I'm in love,' Emily said.

Laura laughed. 'You only *think*? Blimey, that's a first.'

'There's a drawback.'

'Isn't there always?'

'I don't do compromise. And neither should you, come to think of it.'

'We weren't talking about me. Hang on, what's that supposed to mean? Who's a compromise? Spencer?'

A silence, and a sigh, until Emily said, 'No, not really. That came out wrong. I've just been getting this feeling he isn't right for you. But what do I know? If you're happy to tag along being Mr Perfect's arm candy at all those bloody functions, you go for it, girl.'

'You're not making any sense. Spencer and me, we're solid. It's give and take, in any relationship. You should know that.'

Laura sighed. This random conversation wasn't helping her confusion over her feelings for Spencer one bit. The sound she'd heard coming from outside wasn't helping either: heavy footsteps on the gravel, a swishing sound, followed by a *whump*.

She stood up and crept out into the hall, still holding the phone to her ear. Sure enough, a thick dark shadow, narrowing at the top, had formed across the stained-glass panels in the top half of the door – her Christmas tree had arrived. If she hadn't been talking to Emily, she'd have opened the door and called out her thanks, but more footsteps, lighter, told her Clayton had already left – somehow she knew it had been Clayton, not Saul.

'Laura? You there?'

'Yes, yes. Sorry. Someone at the door.'

'Well, go and...'

'It's all right, they've gone now.' Laura returned smartly to the living room and sat down again. 'Look, never mind about my love life – I don't even know how we got on to that. What's the drawback with... what's his name?'

'Alfie.'

'Trendy name.'

'Trendy guy. Maybe a bit *too* trendy.'

Laura's brain made a rapid interpretation. 'Younger than you?'

'Couple of years, yes.'

This could mean anything. Clearly it was more than a couple of years, otherwise Emily would have said.

'And that's the drawback?'

Really, Emily was getting far too fussy. A younger guy? Was she not thinking of the benefits? Although, no doubt she'd already sampled those.

'Of course it's not. He's allergic to dogs.'

'Ah. Isn't there a pill for that, or a spray or something?'

'Nope. His eyes even started watering when he got near my scarf, the one Wilf had been lying on in his bed.'

Laura raised her eyes, as if Emily could see. Only she could go on a date wearing a scarf she'd rescued from the dog's bed.

'So it's Alfie or Wilf? One of them has to go?'

'Yep, and it's not going to be Wilf.'

'I can remember a time,' Laura said, somewhat abstractedly, 'when you said you'd sacrifice anything for love.'

'Yes, well, you live and learn. When do you want me to come and help put your outside lights up?'

'School breaks up tomorrow, so Wednesday, if you're free? You can help me get the tree up as well.'

'I'll make sure I'm free. I'll message when I'm on the way.'

As he crunched back down Laura's drive, Clayton's heart was as heavy as the tree he'd just delivered. She'd suggested Saul bring it tomorrow – Saul! – but he'd seen no point in waiting, nor for anyone to do the job other than himself. He'd meant to schmooze up to the house and quietly leave the tree he'd chosen for her in the porch but, stupidly, he'd underestimated its weight and by the time he'd lugged it up the drive, there'd been no schmoozing about it. He could have put it in the back of the van and driven it up, but then Saul might have been the one to transfer it to the porch. If she should have happened to look out, or come to the door, he'd wanted it to be him she saw, not Saul. Like he needed to make a point.

But she hadn't looked out, as far as he could tell, and even if she had, he doubted she'd have thought anything of it. As for ringing the bell and offering to take the tree indoors, that had never been an option. She'd made her wishes perfectly clear; he'd do himself no favours by ignoring them.

He hadn't felt like this about a woman in ages, not since Annalise, whom he'd broken up with just before his sister came to live with him, although that was so long ago he couldn't remember how he'd felt about her. There had been girlfriends since – perfectly nice, eligible women – but when he wasn't with them he hadn't wondered constantly what they were doing at that precise moment, who they were talking to, what they were wearing, eating, watching on telly. Not like he did with Laura. Every time he saw her, he felt wired for ages afterwards.

Yesterday, after she'd left his house in such a hurry, he'd thrown on his coat and set off at a fast walking pace, in the opposite direction from the one she'd taken. Sitting still, even staying inside, hadn't felt like an option. He'd completed a circuit of the village, fruitlessly taking in the bottom of Charnley Hill in the process, before he strode back to Squirrel Lane. It had been icy cold and pitch black by the time he'd reached home again.

Laura must realise he had feelings for her, and he knew that in some way they were reciprocated. He'd had that confirmed yesterday; the look she'd given him as their hands touched had been one of pure honesty. And then she'd got scared and run away. Well, he'd just have to coax her back. He'd been around for long enough to know that the kind of connection they had didn't come along very often, if at all. It would be a travesty to ignore it, and Laura would see that too, eventually. If she'd been involved with anyone other than Spencer, Clayton might have hidden his feelings away and left her alone. As it was, her being with that man gave him more reason to do the opposite.

Reaching the bottom of Laura's drive now, he jumped into the van, slammed the door shut and revved up unnecessarily loudly. He hoped she could hear, and was thinking about him. Glancing in the mirror, he saw he had a ridiculous grin on his face. Saul was still submerged in his virtual world as the van lurched through the gates. Suddenly he looked up, like he'd only just realised they were moving, and shoved the phone into the top pocket of his jacket as if he wanted rid of it.

'Holly?' Clayton ventured.

'Nope. I heard from her at the weekend. Probably won't hear again now till she's home at the end of the week.'

'But you hoped you might.'

'No reason to get in touch, has she? Not before.'

Saul folded his arms, gazing straight in front of him. Glancing at his tight expression, Clayton could almost see his brain racing around in circles, rationalising Holly's behaviour and forcing it into an acceptable shape to fit in with his own hopes and desires. As you did.

'What about you, then?' Saul said, his eyes still on the road ahead.

'What about me?'

Saul gave a little laugh. 'You know what. You and the famous Mrs Engleby.'

'Laura? Ah, well, she is actually spoken for, if you hadn't noticed.'

'Only by that smooth bastard, Jennings.'

Clayton laughed. 'You don't think he's competition, then?'

They were at the bus stop, Saul's drop-off point. Clayton pulled the van in to the side. Saul undid his seat belt, flung back the door and slithered down.

'Course not. The man's a tool.'

CHAPTER 19

To Laura's relief, the school term had ended two days ago. The pageant had gone remarkably well; off-stage dramas concerning missing ballet shoes, unstuck fake beards and panics over suddenly-forgotten song words had been quickly smoothed over and tears mopped up. Nobody refused to take part at the last minute, and there was none of the deliberate treading on the hem of the child in front, as there had been last year. The pictures on the school's website showed over-excited, happy children, and knackered but smiling teachers. Good result all round, then.

Yesterday, Emily had turned up around midday and she and Laura had worked themselves into a daze fixing up Spindlewood for Christmas, as Emily described it. The outside lights were up, comprising strings of multicoloured bulbs looped above the porch and the downstairs windows, and nets of twinkling silver fairy lights were draped over the bushes at the front of the house. Inside, the mantelpieces and windowsills were filled, fake ivy, embellished with red ribbon bows, wound its way around every picture and mirror, and Holly's miniature houses stood in a circle on a side table. In the hall, the Christmas tree stood guard, lit with hundreds of white lights and a decoration on every branch. It was such a big tree that the tips of Cynthia's wings almost touched the high ceiling but it looked spectacular. Clayton had chosen well.

Laura was experimenting with quiche fillings and delicacies to serve at her party. Tonight, when Spencer came, they'd try out the quiches with homemade potato croquettes, already in the freezer, and a salad. Nice and easy. She'd check the wine later but Spencer would bring some anyway; he'd never shown much enthusiasm for her random stocks of special-offer bottles.

The kitchen windows were steamed up, the warm air fragrant with savoury deliciousness. Laura had just rolled out another sheet of pastry ready to line a fluted quiche tin when she remembered she hadn't paid Clayton for the Christmas tree. She'd hunted amongst the branches for a price tag and found only a thin bit of elastic knotted round the trunk, suggesting the tag had been removed, but she had a rough idea how much it would be. Best do it now, she thought, before she forgot again.

Five minutes later, Laura put on her duffle coat and slipped a wodge of notes into her pocket from the emergency stash in the kitchen drawer. Then, as an afterthought, she filled a small plastic bag with miniature cheese scones, flavoured with herbs and paprika, from the cooling rack, and put that in her other pocket.

As she closed the front door, her feet stalled on the step. Clayton's van was approaching. She hadn't seen him to speak to since Monday and she'd felt awkward enough then. The walk down to the tree sales plot would have given her breathing space to compose herself and arrange her thoughts. But now, here he was, stopping the van at the top of the drive and grinning at her through the windscreen.

'Hey,' he said, opening the door and jumping down.

'I was coming down. You must've read my mind.'

'It's one of my many talents.'

His gaze met hers, and stayed there. *No, not today. Please.* Tearing her gaze away, Laura slid her hand into her pocket and brought out the money.

'Now,' she said, in her most businesslike voice, 'how much do I owe you?'

'Owe me? What for?'

'The tree, of course.'

'Is it what you wanted?'

'It's perfect.'

'It's a present. For saving the day.' Clayton directed a thumb over his shoulder.

'No, no. You've paid me quite enough for the use of the garden.'

She fumbled with the money. A twenty-pound note fluttered to the ground. She stooped to retrieve it but Clayton was already there, scooping it up. As they stood up, the tops of their heads brushed one another. Laura caught the scent of fresh air, pine needles and shampoo.

Clayton held out the note to her.

'No,' she said. 'I want to pay. It wouldn't feel right otherwise. Tell me how much it is altogether.'

Clayton hesitated, then nodded. He named an amount which was obviously far less than the tree was worth but as much as he was prepared to accept. 'Otherwise,' he added, 'we could be here all day, arguing the toss.'

The rest of the money changed hands. Laura remembered the scones, and handed those over too. 'For you and Saul to share.'

'Thanks. Did you want something doing, while I'm here? I see the ladder's up.'

Laura followed his line of sight. 'Oh, no, that's there from yesterday. Emily and I put the lights up.'

'Shall I put the ladder away for you, then? I was going round to the shed.'

'Yes, please,' Laura said, happy to accept his help, now that the matter of paying for the tree had been settled. 'That would be very kind.'

Clayton's eyebrows lifted, the twitch of his lips betraying amusement at her attempt at formality. Really, he was incorrigible. But knowing that didn't stop her from following him round the back of the house and across the garden to the sheds. She opened the door of the unlocked shed where the ladder was kept, and Clayton stowed it neatly inside before unlocking the second shed.

'The landlord of the Goose wants a Noble, a five-footer. I put this one by for him. I'm going to drop it in on my way home,' Clayton said, dragging the tree out.

'Shall I help?'

'No, you're all right.' The tree, imprisoned in its mesh shroud, had already made the easy journey to Clayton's shoulder. 'Lock up, though, if you like.'

He threw her the key. She fielded it neatly, locked the shed and followed Clayton round to the front of the house.

'You've got pine needles stuck in your sweater,' she said, when the tree had been stowed in the van.

'Have I?' Clayton gave his shoulder a perfunctory brush. 'You've got flour in your hair, and some on your face.'

'I've been baking.'

She was going to add 'for my party', before she remembered he wouldn't be there, and felt sad.

'I'd better get back, then,' Clayton said, making no attempt to move.

Laura didn't want him to go. Even though he was only going as far as the end of her garden, she really didn't want him to go.

Spencer, she made herself think. *Spencer*. She repeated the name inside her head, like a mantra.

Clayton gave a little nod and walked towards the van. Suddenly, he stopped and turned round.

'Could I take you to dinner at the Goose? One night soon?'

Laura's mouth dried. The words took some effort to form. 'You really don't need to do that. We're all square, really...'

'It's nothing to do with me using your garden. I'd really like to, that's all.' He smiled. 'What d'you say?' It sounded like a challenge.

'Clayton, I can't. I'm sorry.'

He nodded slowly. 'Well, I could say we had coffee at the Ginger Cat, so why not dinner at the Goose, but that wouldn't be a fair comparison. I could also say I wasn't asking you out on a date, but we both know I'd be lying.'

'And we both know I'm seeing someone,' Laura said quietly.

'Laura, can I ask you something?' Clayton didn't wait for a reply. 'How well do you really know Spencer Jennings?'

She shrugged. 'How well do we really know anybody?'

Laura looked across the dining table at Spencer, who was studiously eating tiny pieces of quiche from the selection she'd put on his plate. She'd almost forgotten why she'd made all this food now, let alone asked Spencer to try it. Her mind was in turmoil. Her chest ached with the effort of holding it all in and carrying on as if everything was fine.

Why had Clayton thought it was all right to ask her out when he knew full well she was in a relationship? And what had he meant by that odd question about Spencer?

'Definitely this one,' Spencer was saying. 'It has a really refined taste.'

'What? Oh yes, the one with the red peppers,' Laura said, hauling her mind back to the present. 'Came out well, I thought.'

'Actually,' Spencer said, 'I like them all.' He indicated the plate. 'These two seem the same, though. Are they?'

'Different cheese.'

'Ah. Well, whichever you serve on Christmas Eve, they'll go down a storm, and so will the baby scones, the chicken curry puffs and the herby rice balls. They're all delicious. You are clever, Laura.'

Smiling, Spencer set aside his plate, drank some of his wine and put down the glass in a determined way. Until then, Laura had forgotten he'd said he wanted to talk to her; her preoccupation with other matters had seen to that. She picked up her glass. It contained only dregs. She seemed to be drinking more than usual tonight. Spencer reached for the bottle and topped up her glass.

'Here's to us,' he said, clinking his glass against hers.

'Cheers.'

'I've been thinking a lot lately, about us.'

'Have you?' Laura drank more wine, too fast. It gave her a head rush; she realised she'd hardly eaten a thing.

'We make a good team, don't you think?' Spencer's smile lasered across the table.

What sort of a question was that?

'I suppose we do.'

Spencer seemed unfazed by her vagueness, unless he hadn't noticed it. 'If you'd like me to, I could stay over after the party and be with you on Christmas Day, instead of flogging all the way to Gloucestershire. I have to leave at the crack of dawn to get there in time for lunch and the roads are bound to be icy.'

Laura frowned. 'Spence, you know you'd be welcome to stay

over Christmas, but wouldn't your parents be upset? They must be looking forward to seeing you.'

'Oh, I'm sure they'd understand.'

Laura wasn't so sure about that, but never mind. 'Was that what you wanted to talk to me about?'

'Yes. And no, not really.'

'What then?'

Spencer took a moment, seemingly making up his mind about something. 'Well, yes, that's it for now. Perhaps you'll give it some thought. About me being here with you through Christmas, I mean.'

'Yes, of course. But it's not just up to me, is it?'

There was something more on Spencer's mind than deciding where he was to spend Christmas, she could tell. His pensive silence underlined that. She waited.

He reached across, touched her hand briefly, then withdrew it. 'Perhaps this year we could make the Christmas Eve party something special. One to remember?'

'My parties are always memorable,' Laura said, deliberately misunderstanding.

The nerves in her stomach were starting to jangle. She drank some more wine, then swiftly put her glass down and pushed it out of reach as the head rush came back with more force. She picked up a triangle of quiche and took a bite.

Spencer smiled but his eyes were serious. 'You do love me, don't you?'

She returned the smile. 'You know I do.'

Yes. Now she'd said it out loud, the doubts floated away, like a balloon set free. She loved Spencer, had done for a long time. He was a lovely man and she was lucky to have been given this second chance. And now, if she was reading him correctly, he wanted them to make more of a commitment, which could mean he was going to suggest moving in together, or even... was he planning a Christmas Eve proposal? How romantic! Her stomach skittered again, but this time it was from excitement, not nerves.

But was that what she wanted? Living together, providing it was here at Spindlewood, might be fun, and good for them both. But marriage? Unlikely though it seemed, she hadn't even thought about marrying Spencer. How would she answer, should he propose on Christmas Eve? She really had no idea.

'I am happy with us, with the way we are,' she said, hearing a slight note of panic in her voice. 'Aren't you?'

Spencer tapped the side of his nose. 'Let's just wait and see, shall we?'

Wait and see, repeated Laura's wine-misted brain. In ten days from now, it would be Christmas Eve and Clayton Masters would be gone from her property, taking her confused thoughts and distractions with him, and all would become clear.

CHAPTER 20

On Monday, Emily left the square, glass-fronted building, home of the *Cliffhaven News*, and walked slowly across the forecourt to the staff parking bays. Her head felt muzzy, her eyes gritty from staring at the screen all morning. She was supposed to have been writing up a piece about the controversial new sewage works at Cliffhaven, but once she'd started delving, she hadn't been able to stop. Getting into the car, she took her lunchtime sandwich from her bag, then changed her mind about eating it there and put it on the passenger seat before starting the engine.

Ten minutes later, after a distracted drive through the town during which she'd been tooted at twice, she arrived at the car park on top of the cliff. There was only one other car there, and hardly anyone else about. It was perishing cold with a biting wind; not the best sort of day for a clifftop walk, but she needed the air to clear her head. Locking the car, she pulled up the hood of her parka and tightened the strings before setting out along the tufted grass, taking care to stay well back from the fence and its warning signs.

The granite-grey sea rolled and crashed. A tanker brushed a

dark shape on the choppy horizon. *I saw three ships come sailing in* insisted Emily's anxious mind. *On Christmas Day, on Christmas Day*. Should she tell Laura what she'd found out about Spencer? Come clean about the way she'd tricked him into revealing his real name and pass on the results of her morning's research, which would be even more devastating? It would ruin Laura's Christmas. But maybe it was better than waiting until she'd done something stupid like getting herself engaged to the bloke.

On Saturday, Emily and Laura had driven to Lewes, then taken the train into Brighton for some last-minute Christmas shopping. Last-minute for Laura, that was; her friend usually had all her presents wrapped and labelled by the first week in December, whereas Emily's own idea of last-minute was a dash round the shops half an hour before they closed on Christmas Eve.

Over lunch in The Lanes, Laura had gone all sparkly-eyed and giggly, which wasn't like her. If anyone had both feet on the ground, it was Laura. Emily hadn't known what to say when she'd heard about the 'special' Christmas Eve Spencer had hinted at. She'd always encouraged Laura's relationship with Spencer, admittedly with her fingers metaphorically crossed behind her back – she'd never been totally convinced he was good enough for Laura; he was too controlling, in Emily's opinion. But if her friend was happy, who was she to go spoiling things?

But now...

Since the date that never was, Emily had been wondering whether Spencer was hiding behind a façade. And then, there were Laura's remarks about the boring business functions, and Spencer's expectations as to what she wore and how she should look. She might have spoken with a good dose of humour, but none of this boded well for their future relationship.

She'd played down Laura's news and advised her not to rush

into anything, especially not at Christmas, a time of heightened, and possibly unreal, emotions.

'You're right, Em,' Laura had said, when she'd stopped sparkling. 'Don't worry, I won't be coerced into doing anything I don't want to do. Actually, I don't know if I want to get married again, and there's Holly to consider. But it's nice to be asked, isn't it?'

Emily had relented then, and they'd ordered a bottle of elderflower fizz and had a good old giggle about men and romances, past and present.

But that was then. Before Emily knew that Spencer Jennings was really Marcus Dartnell, the man who had caused Louise Masters' death and lied his way out of it. Okay, that was never proven, but Clayton must have been pretty sure, as was the journalist who'd obviously spoken to him and then written up the article in one of the nationals after the court case was over. From what Emily had read in the newspaper archives, doubts over Spencer's – or rather, Marcus's – version of events had been scattered like daisies across a hundred acre field. Opinion didn't count without facts, but mud stuck where it was thrown.

It explained everything: the mysterious mention of 'history' between Spencer and Clayton, his insistence that Laura should have nothing more to do with Clayton, the row between the two men in the Goose and Feather, and – Emily had only just thought of this – Spencer's failure to introduce Laura to his parents and brother.

He must have been horrified when he discovered Clayton was Laura's gardener, and that he'd be setting up shop at Spindlewood for weeks on end, never mind having to face him over the development site dispute. He must be on tenterhooks, wondering if, and when, Clayton would present Laura with his side of the story. Presumably, as Clayton had said nothing to Laura so far, he wouldn't be doing so. That little task had fallen to Emily, although how she was going to break the news she had no idea.

Emily stopped walking and stood gazing out to sea. The tanker had moved east, a distant smudge. The line of the horizon was barely visible, grey on grey; it could be raining out there. The wind stung her eyes. She wiped them with her gloved hand, then headed back towards the warm sanctuary of the car.

Monday morning, and Laura was making mince pies to go in the freezer, in case Holly didn't get round to it.

The university term had finished on Friday, and Laura had waited all of Saturday, expecting her daughter either to put in an appearance or ring to let her know what was going on. By Sunday morning there was still no word. Not wanting to play the part of the worrying, clingy mother, Laura had waited until ten and then she'd rung Holly.

'Sorry, Mum,' Holly had mumbled through a headful of sleep. 'There was a party last night. I thought I said. Didn't I say?'

'No, you didn't,' Laura had said, feeling disappointed. Hearing Holly's voice, she was missing her now. 'It doesn't matter, as long as you're all right. Did you have a good time?'

'Great.' Laura detected a sigh, or it could've been a yawn. 'Listen, Mum, would you mind if I stopped on here a bit longer? Only there's stuff happening, but I'll be down in a couple of days.'

'Stuff? What kind of stuff?'

'Oh, you know, just stuff.'

How enlightening, Laura had thought. Did all students on the English course have as limited a vocabulary?

'Are you cool with that, Mum?'

Laura had stifled a disappointed sigh. 'Yes, I'm cool with that.

Enjoy the... *stuff*, and when you do get back, ring if you need a lift from the station.'

It was only a few more days. They'd have plenty of time together when Holly did eventually get herself home. Laura floured and rolled and cut and filled. Holly always made star shapes to go on the tops of the pies. Laura always made rounds, twisting the point of a knife in the pastry to let the steam out, but today she made stars.

Later, she eyed the baked pies with satisfaction. They were the perfect shade of pale gold. The aroma of buttery pastry and rich, spicy mincemeat from one of the jars she'd bought in the village filled the kitchen; the essence of Christmas. She picked up a pie and took a bite, then waved a hand in front of her mouth as the hot mincemeat scorched her tongue. Delicious, though.

She cleared up from the baking, leaving the mixing bowl to soak in the sink, and made a coffee. Peering through the steamed-up kitchen window, she watched the trees at the top of the garden sweeping back and forth in the strengthening wind, their branches scratching patterns against a forbidding-looking sky. It had rained heavily in the night, and more rain was forecast. She hoped the weather people were wrong; Clayton and Saul had enough to contend with, being outside with only that flimsy tarpaulin for shelter. Sometimes they sat in the van; she'd seen them do that.

Finishing her coffee, Laura wandered upstairs to the turret room. The windows were rattling quite violently. Most of the upstairs windows rattled, but these were the worst because the position of the turret on the corner of the house meant that it caught the full force of the weather.

She noticed the wall was damp beneath the central window. Not just damp – a section of the wall was really wet and rainwater had run down and soaked into the carpet.

Stooping to investigate further, she prised the carpet away from the wall and peeled it up. The floorboards were wet. This must have been going on for a while, and last night's downpour had added to the problem. She examined the windowsills. They needed replacing, inside and out; that would have to wait a while longer, but she could plug the gaps in the meantime. To do that properly she'd have to wait until it was dry again, but a little emergency repair work was certainly in order.

The rain had already begun when, ten minutes later, Laura fastened back the door of the smaller shed while she scouted about amongst the boxes and general clutter. Filler. There used to be some. She'd had to use that before, on the bathroom sill. And wood; she could fix a piece of wooden beading across the top of the sill. It would look awful but a bodge-up job was all she had time for right now. Nobody went to the turret room except her, and anyway what did looks matter as long as the rain was kept out? A crusty-looking tub of filler revealed itself from the shelf containing old tins of paint. The lid was stuck fast. Laura located a screwdriver and attacked the lid. It came away suddenly, bringing a gloop of grey filler with it which promptly spread itself over her hand.

'Damn!'

'Are you okay in there?'

Laura turned to find Clayton in the doorway. He was wearing a grey beanie hat, pulled well down over his forehead; it made him look like a young, very cute, mugger. Laura stifled a giggle.

'Yes, thanks. I'm going to use some of this. Or I was, if there's enough left.' She examined her sticky hand and made a face.

'Can I do it for you, whatever it is?' Clayton said, stepping inside the shed.

'It's awful out there,' she said, ignoring Clayton's question as she looked past him at the rain, which was now virtually horizontal as the wind carried it. 'You can't stand out in this, selling Christmas trees. You'll have to pack up.'

'We've been out in worse. Saul's in the van, but yes, I think we'll give it up for today. The punters won't be rushing up here in this.' He thumbed towards the other shed. 'I came to get some more twine to bind up the trees but I don't think I'll bother now. So what was it you were planning on doing with the gunk?'

Laura explained about the window, and the piece of wood she might use as well, although there didn't seem to be anything suitable in here, and goodness knows where the wood glue was.

'I can do it,' she said, in case Clayton thought otherwise. 'I just need the right equipment.'

'Which is where I can help, if you'll let me,' he said. 'I'll drop Saul off, nip back to mine and come back with the necessaries this afternoon. I'll soon have it fixed. No point in you doing it, unless you've got a burning desire?'

Laura almost blushed, but held it back. She wished he wouldn't use expressions like that. Having Clayton fix the window would be useful, though; she had other plans for this afternoon, including wrapping the presents she'd bought in Brighton on Saturday. On the other hand, perhaps it wasn't such a good idea...

'No strings,' Clayton said, correctly interpreting her hesitation. 'I said before I'd do some stuff around the house, and I'd be happy to help out, especially in an emergency. And now I'm free for the rest of the day...?'

Laura smiled. 'Well, then, if you're really sure, yes please. I would be grateful.'

'Great. I'll need to do a recce of the site first, if that's all right with you.'

Was this wise, Laura thought, as the two of them made a dash through the rain to the house? But he'd said *no strings*; that oblique reference was his way of telling her he knew where he stood, so there shouldn't be any awkwardness between them after his failed invitation to dinner.

'Oh, wow.' Clayton gazed around the turret room, after they'd dripped up the stairs. 'I've never been inside a circular room before, except in a castle. Great view of the garden. The light coming in from all sides is fantastic.'

'It's my special place,' Laura said.

Clayton nodded, understanding. She showed him the problem with the window. She'd peeled the carpet back further and tucked an old bath towel into the space. It was already damp. Clayton's inspection only took a few minutes, then he was bounding down the stairs and out of the front door with a promise to come back in around an hour.

Back in the dining room, she wrapped the red cashmere sweater she'd bought for Spencer, and Emily's present, a pendant with a smoky blue stone she'd admired when they were in Brighton – Laura had sneaked into the shop and bought it. After a while, she noticed that the rain no longer hammered at the windows, the wind had dropped and the sky had lightened in places to an optimistic diluted blue. How quickly everything changed. This afternoon, Clayton would come to fix the window. Afterwards she'd give him tea and a mince pie in the kitchen, and they'd be back to how they were before.

Clayton sat in the Goose and Feather, his pint in front of him. It was his second drink. The alcohol and the warmth from the log fire were doing a great job in mellowing his mood, as was the casual banter being exchanged around the bar; he'd been slightly on edge when he'd got home from Laura's.

From the back room came the click of billiard balls and the strident voices of Charnley Acre's younger residents. Saul was amongst them. He still had a thing for Holly Engleby – he'd thrown her name into the conversation enough times for Clayton to catch on to that. Well, the girl would be home soon. If she was anything like her mother, Saul would have to up his game if he wanted to date her.

Which was exactly what Clayton himself intended to do with Laura.

He'd behaved with great restraint today, he thought, privately congratulating himself. He'd enjoyed fixing the window – a temporary fix but it should see her through the rest of the winter. He'd do anything to help Laura, he really would. He'd fix up the whole damn house if she would let him, the bits that were within his scope, anyway. She'd been very grateful for the window repair, and, of course, she'd insisted on paying him. Knowing she'd feel more comfortable if he took something, he'd accepted the rough cost of the materials he'd used, and a little on top. He'd politely turned down her offer of tea, pretending he had something to rush off for, although the only place he'd wanted to be right then was in Laura's kitchen, having a cosy chat at her table. The swift look of disappointment in her eyes was reward enough for his sacrifice. The connection was still there. All he had to do was to find a way through her determination to keep him at arm's length.

All. Yeah, right. Clayton laughed softly to himself.

'Share the joke then,' came from the next table.

'Nothing you'd find funny,' he said.

Actually, he was remembering what Saul had said about Spencer – Marcus – being no competition, and a 'tool' as well. Right on both counts.

Clayton looked towards the door of the pub, almost willing Spencer to walk in. Although the sight of the man, and especially the thought of him with Laura, made him feel physically sick, he quite liked the idea of giving him a filthy look, a proper facing. The door continued to swing as customers came and went, but no Spencer. Perhaps he was up at Spindlewood, with Laura in his deceitful arms, right at this moment. Clayton downed the rest of his pint fast, to dispel the image.

Talking of upping his game, perhaps he should come clean and tell Laura, straight out, how he felt about her. He'd never been shy with women before, so why start now? Okay, Laura was obviously a woman of integrity; she wasn't the two-timing type, which meant that in order to go out with him, she'd have to give Spencer the old heave-ho first. He had to leave her space and time to do that, didn't he? He couldn't expect to get a 'yes' straight away. Given her kindheartedness she was hardly likely to dump Spencer so close to Christmas.

If he was to stand any chance of success with Laura, he must be patient, play the waiting game and see how things panned out. He wouldn't wait too long, though. Just long enough for her to regret having turned him down. Just long enough for her to realise where her true affections lay – with him, not with that lying, jumped-up, toffee-nosed apology for a man.

The thud of darts hitting the board a few feet away jolted Clayton's mind back to reality. It wasn't going to happen, was it? Him and Laura. He was living in a dream world. Anyway, how come he'd gone and fallen in love when he'd had no intention of doing that again for the foreseeable, because he'd decided his life was absolutely fine as it was? *Fallen in love*. Now, there was a thing... Chuckling softly at his own daftness, Clayton picked up his glass and realised it was empty. Another? Or should he get off home now? Somehow, the thought of turning the key and opening the door onto a silent, empty house didn't appeal. He got up and went to the bar.

CHAPTER 21

Saul was in a quandary.

They'd packed up selling the trees at lunchtime on Monday because of the foul weather. This was after he'd been left sitting like a prune in the steamed up van for an absolute age while Clayton was up at the shed fetching more twine, which he'd then come back without – Saul hadn't asked but it didn't take his three A levels to work out what, or rather who, had kept him.

While he'd waited for Clayton, he hadn't wasted his time. He'd sent Holly a text: *Hiya, any idea when you'll be back in the sticks?* All casual, like he wasn't that bothered. She'd replied gratifyingly fast: *Some time Wednesday. Lk fwd to a catchup. H.*

Wednesday? He'd expected her before that, considering her term had ended, but the message had sounded promising, like she really wanted to see him. And now it was Wednesday afternoon, and Laura had gone to Lewes Station to meet Holly – he'd heard her tell Clayton when she stopped to speak to him before she drove out of the gates. By Saul's reckoning, they should be back at any minute. But what then? No doubt they'd drive straight up to the house. Should he wait a while for her to get settled, then nip up there, say 'hi' and welcome her home, sort of thing? Or might that seem uncool, or even – perish the thought – a bit desperate? Anyway, there'd be little chance of talking to her properly with her mother there.

The alternatives weren't that attractive either. If he waited until tomorrow, she'd probably make her way down to the tree site at some point, but then he'd have Clayton within earwigging distance, not to mention half the village. It seemed kind of important that if – when – he asked Holly out on a date, he did it face to face, in private.

Saul sighed inwardly as he scooped eight hot chestnuts into a bag and exchanged them for a quid. If only Holly wasn't so important to him, he could just go with the flow. But the more he'd thought about what had happened between them back in October, the more she'd sashayed her way into his head, and his heart. Their reunion – and the beginning of what was to come – had to be perfect. He had to get it right. The problem was, he wasn't too sure how to manage that. Clearly the matter required a lot more serious thought.

'Mum, I've met somebody, at uni,' Holly said, once the back seat of the car was piled with her rucksack and stuff, and they'd done the did-you-have-a-good-journey conversation.

'Have you, darling? Who is he?'

Her mum was concentrating on the road as they left Lewes, looking dead front and not at Holly, but her smile said she wasn't taking this news as seriously as she might have done.

And so Holly told her all about Lorcan, and how close they'd become in such a short time, and how very special he was, and how very special their relationship was. She didn't add that she was already missing him like crazy and she had no idea how she was going to survive the Christmas holidays without seeing him. They were going to Facetime, Skype, whatever, but she suspected that might make her feel even worse, knowing he was so far away, in the middle of bloody Wales.

'He sounds lovely,' her mum said. 'I take it this Lorcan has some connection to you not coming down right after the end of term?'

'Might do.' Holly couldn't suppress a smile.

'Well, I hope you're treating him properly. And he you, of course.'

'What's that supposed to mean?'

'It *means*... oh, I don't know.'

Mum flapped a hand, causing the bloke driving a Mondeo on the outside lane to throw her a confused look, like he thought she was doing some sort of hand signal.

The Mondeo driver tooted. 'Prat,' Holly's mum said.

'No, go on.' Her mother clearly had something on her mind.

'Saul Fielding. He asked when you were coming home. And he was listening in when I mentioned to Clayton I was coming to fetch you and making no secret of it.'

'So?'

'You had a bit of a thing with him in reading week, didn't you? And don't ask me how I know. I just do.'

Holly sighed. 'It wasn't a *thing*. We hung out a bit, that's all, but no more than I did with everyone else.'

Not quite true, but she wasn't going to share the juicier details with her mother. Neither would this be the time to mention Saul's texts; her mother clearly had the bit between her teeth on this one.

'It doesn't matter. Forget I said anything – it's nothing to do with me. Only you know he's at Spindlewood, don't you? Saul. Standing in our garden right at this minute?'

Holly nodded. 'Selling Christmas trees or something. You did say.'

'Just be careful, Holly, that's all. If he's sweet on you it wouldn't be fair to lead him on, especially with Lorcan in the picture.'

'Honestly, Mum,' Holly said, laughing. 'I do have some scruples you know.'

Her mum's turn to laugh. 'Good, well keep it that way.'

They were home now, the car swinging off the hill and in through the gates that were kept permanently open. Holly smiled. Spindlewood looked so pretty, so welcoming, and the lights were up for Christmas even though they weren't switched on. She loved coming home. Wherever she was in the world, she would always look forward to coming back to Spindlewood.

'Shall we stop?' Mum said, glancing at her. 'Your decision.'

In one sweep of her gaze, Holly took in rows of Christmas trees filling a large area of the lawn, a hot chestnut brazier, and a tent thing at the back, where Clayton was standing. And there was Saul, too, kind of looking right at her but kind of pretending he wasn't. Her stomach tightened, just a tiny bit; she'd forgotten how handsome he was.

'Yes. Stop.'

Mum stood on the brake. Clayton came up to her window as she lowered it and said 'hello' to both of them, although he must have seen her mum less than half an hour ago. That was some smile he gave her, Holly was amused to note. He was just a bit gorgeous, for an old guy, even with that daft hat on. She'd never spotted that before.

Saul came up behind Clayton. She beckoned him round and lowered her window. 'Hiya.'

'Hi. Welcome home.'

'Ta. See you down the Goose some time, I expect.'

'Yep, you can rely on it.'

Another car had come up behind theirs, two in fact. People coming to buy Christmas trees, no doubt.

'Good to have you back, Holly,' Saul added, stepping back as the car pulled away.

Her mum was right; she would have to be careful there. But she'd already known that without being told. She could see Saul in the rear-view mirror, standing half in the drive and looking in the direction of the car. Extra careful, then.

She was home. And he'd spoken to her. She'd looked worn out; it was a long journey from Birmingham – two trains, one to London, then one down to Lewes – so it wasn't surprising. In a way, the few words they'd exchanged had left him in a kind of limbo. It hadn't been enough to suss out whether she was especially pleased to see him or if she was just being friendly. He mustn't expect too much too soon, though.

'She's back then,' Clayton observed unnecessarily, widening his eyes meaningfully at Saul.

'Obviously.'

Saul raised his eyes, and turned his attention to a middle-aged couple who'd just climbed down from their Range Rover and were inspecting the trees. He knew them slightly because they were friends of his parents. After they'd paid for their tree and it had made its way into the back of the Range Rover, he gave them each a bag of chestnuts for free, because Clayton had said they were calling it a day soon. It was perishing cold, admittedly, and the sky overhead had turned the colour of a day-old bruise. At least if he was off the premises, there'd be no chance of him hoofing it up to the house to chase down Holly, which he knew now would be totally the wrong thing to do.

They packed up in double-quick time, and as they drove

away in the van, Saul turned and glanced back at the house, but there was no sign of Holly. Clayton must have noticed him looking.

'You do know it would be the same every time she went away, don't you? Worrying yourself sick over who she's with and what she's doing when she's gone. Driving yourself mad every time she's due back. Find yourself a nice local girl, I would.'

Thinking about Laura, Saul was going to say *like you have, you mean*, but thought better of it. Clayton and Laura weren't even seeing each other, as far as he knew, although you'd never know it from the way they acted when they were together.

Instead, he said: 'We'll see,' while he wondered if his blue shirt had been through the wash yet, the one Holly had once said matched his eyes. She'd been sober at the time. Well, almost.

CHAPTER 22

The following morning, Laura eyed the number of patty tins waiting on the kitchen table while Holly flopped a vast lump of pastry around the mixing bowl. A jar of mincemeat stood ready, with a spoon stuck in it.

'I hope you aren't making too many pies,' Laura said. 'I put dozens in the freezer the other day.'

Holly looked suspiciously at her. 'Round lids?'

'Stars.'

Holly smiled approvingly. 'Making pastry's therapeutic. I need therapy after pumping out all those essays.'

Laura swerved around Holly and switched the kettle on again. She was chain-drinking coffee, which wasn't healthy, but she seemed to be having trouble concentrating at the moment.

'I could do cheese straws as well?'

'Yes, do. Yours are always better than mine.'

'This is true,' Holly said. A cloud of flour rose as she slapped the pastry onto the board.

Laura's phone rang. She picked it up from the windowsill.

'I have to talk to you,' Emily said. She sounded as if she'd been running.

'Go on then, I'm listening.'

'No, not now. In person. Can you come to mine, around twelve? I should be home by then.'

'Yes, if you like... Em, are you all right? Has something happened? You sound funny.'

'I'm fine. I'll explain all when I see you. Oh, and don't bring the car.'

'Why on earth not?'

'Because you're going to need a drink.'

Laura gripped the arms of the chair and stared across Emily's living room, not at Emily, but past her, towards the window. But she wasn't seeing anything except a muzzy square of white light. All this time, and she hadn't a clue that the man she was seeing – had fallen in love with – was actually somebody quite different. Somebody who, at the time of the incident on the country road, had thought only of himself and not of what – or who – he might have hit. Somebody who had not accepted any blame, nor shown remorse. He'd even had the effrontery to come back to Charnley Acre after his sojourn in Gloucestershire and carry on regardless. Carry on, in fact, as if he owned the place, which was how he behaved sometimes, only she'd seen that as confidence, not arrogance.

Spencer must have known Clayton still lived in the village, or he could have found out, yet he was prepared to risk causing him more pain just because it suited him to return to the area.

'He even changed his name,' she said, looking at Emily. 'I had no idea.'

'Why would you? He must have taken a chance that nobody in Charnley Acre apart from Clayton would remember that far back and recognise him as being involved in the case. Or maybe he just didn't care.'

Laura felt the swell of tears in her throat, but they wouldn't come. It might have been better if they had, but she was too shocked, too angry, to release them. She thought about Clayton. Every time he saw Spencer it must remind him of the tragedy – not that he could forget. He could so easily have told her the whole story but he hadn't because he knew what it would do to her. Clayton cared about her; she could no longer ignore that, and neither could she go on pretending his feelings weren't reciprocated.

Emily went quietly to the kitchen and came back with two gin and tonics, clinking with ice. She put one into Laura's hand. She sipped it, sipped some more. It slid down like liquid fire.

'Heavens, how much gin have you put in this?'

'It's medicinal.' Emily returned to her chair. 'I'll make us some pasta to soak it up in a minute.'

'I might've agreed for us to live together, had he asked. I was tempted,' Laura said. 'Knowing what I know now, I think that was going to be Spencer's party surprise, not a proposal.'

'Yep, getting married would've been a trifle awkward with him living under an assumed name,' Emily said.

'God, yes. On the other hand, perhaps he'd already got that part worked out.'

'That's why I had to tell you now, before the party. I didn't want to spoil your Christmas and I'm really sorry if I have, but you see why it couldn't wait.'

Laura flapped a hand. 'You did right to tell me and I'll be fine. I'm made of tougher stuff than Spencer gives me credit for, that I do know.'

Wilf padded into the room and settled down contentedly beside Emily's chair. She reached down and fondled the old dog's ears.

They sat in contemplative silence for a while, until Emily looked up at Laura and said, 'What're you going to do?'

'Do?' Laura was surprised by the question. She hadn't thought that far. 'I'll confront him, of course. I'll tell him what I know and then I'll show him the door.'

It felt strangely liberating to be saying that. Sad, too, though, at what had been lost. She had loved Spencer, and probably a tiny bit of her still did. Or rather, she'd loved the man she'd thought he was. Maybe he'd loved her too, in his own way.

And then there was Clayton. What about him? Should she talk to him, too, and tell him she knew the story? She couldn't decide that now. It was all too raw, too unnerving. One step at a time.

CHAPTER 23

At eight o'clock in the morning, before she got out of bed, Laura reached for her phone and sent Spencer a text: *I'm coming over this morning. Please be in. I need to talk to you.*

As she lay back on the pillows, his reply pinged through: *Great. I'm in all morning. Love you. x*

Typical, Laura thought. He hadn't spotted any signs in her curt message that all might not be well, which to anyone else would have been as plain as daylight. Speaking of which... Laura studied the strangely luminous brightness of the slice of ceiling above the window. In seconds she was out of bed, and throwing back the curtains. Snow! Her eyes widened at the astonishing spectacle of the garden, transformed overnight into a white wonderland. The bedroom door burst open and Holly bounced in wearing pyjama shorts and an ancient Snoopy sweatshirt she'd had since she was thirteen.

'It's snowed!' She leapt across the room, via Laura's bed, to land next to her at the window.

'Yep, it's snowed. And it still is, a bit. See those tiny flakes?'

'Snow fairies,' Holly said. 'We must tell Cynthia.'

Laura put an arm round Holly and squeezed her shoulders. 'I'm so glad you're here.'

Holly raised her eyes. 'Where else would I be? Don't go all soft on me in your old age, Mother.'

They stood together at the window, in awe of the brand-new landscape. The sudden arrival of the snow seemed appropriate somehow, Laura thought, as if it had been sent to blank out all the bad stuff. Yesterday, she'd allowed herself time and space to let her thoughts run free as she'd acclimatised to the new situation. She'd spent the day with her daughter, taking her shopping and for lunch; enjoying having her home again. Today it was time for action. Time to face up to what was to come.

But how was she to get to Spencer's house, way across the other side of Charnley Acre? She wouldn't be driving in this, that was for sure. She wished she'd looked out of the window before she'd told him to expect her but there was nothing she could do about that now.

'Mum, what about the Christmas trees?' Holly said suddenly. 'There's so much snow down there I could hardly make out where they were from my window.'

Laura's window overlooked the back garden; she'd been so caught up in the beauty of the snowy scene that for the moment she'd forgotten about the tree plot. She looked at Holly, then dived for her phone.

'Clayton? It's me. It's been snowing!'

A muffled laugh, then: 'Funnily enough it's done it here, too. Who'd have thought?'

'Yes, but it's *really* deep up here. Everything's smothered. What about the Christmas trees?'

'I know. I'll be there as soon as I can.'

Laura and Holly had breakfast, then layered up in warm clothes and wellington boots before heading outside. The further down the drive they walked, the thicker the snow became. Great mounds of it were banked up around the shrubs, and there was no distinction between the drive, the lawn and the flower beds. The Green and Fragrant van was just turning slowly in at the gate, with Clayton and Saul inside. Snow chains had been fitted to the van's wheels. As it stopped and Clayton jumped out, Laura's stomach swerved. She'd thought she was okay, but now, seeing Clayton, she felt wobbly and hollowed out, as if she'd been crying all night.

Clayton, Saul and Holly tramped around the remaining Christmas trees, the snow almost up to the tops of their boots. Holly stumbled, reached for one of the trees for support and almost pulled it down on top of her, snow from its branches cascading onto her red pom-pom hat. She shrieked with laughter. Laughing too, Saul stood the tree up again, whilst holding onto Holly's arm at the same time. The pair of them slid around in the snow, clutching arms, still laughing. Clayton grinned at Laura, widening his eyes. Feeling more settled, she smiled back.

'I've listened to the forecast on *Cuckmere Sounds*,' Saul said, finally putting some space between him and Holly, 'and there's a weather warning out for more snow later. Nobody in their right mind's going to tackle the hill even if the gritters do manage to get here which means we're stuck with this lot.' He nodded at the trees.

There weren't too many left, Laura noted, but the cost of them mounted up. If Clayton didn't shift his entire stock, she suspected it would cut significantly into his profits.

'No problem, we'll take them back to my place,' he said, rubbing his gloved hands together. 'Anybody who wants one can walk round. I can fit in what's left at the side of my house, in front of the garage.'

Laura, Saul and Holly looked doubtfully at one another, and then at the former sales pitch, now knee-deep in snow. And then they all turned, including Clayton, to see Emily scrunching up from the gate, her face all pink and her breath puffing out in clouds.

'What the...?' Laura began.

Emily came up to her side. 'I didn't hear from you yesterday and I wanted to make sure you were all right, after...' she half-whispered.

'Oh, Em, that's so sweet of you to trek all the way up here. I'm okay though, honestly.'

She hadn't lowered her voice. The others, Clayton included, turned interested faces in her direction.

'Mum?' Holly said.

'I'm fine. It's nothing.' Laura pasted on a smile, and looked pointedly at Emily. 'Now you're here, you can lend a hand shifting this lot.'

Clayton started to protest that he and Saul could manage. But it was snowing again, fat flakes curling out of an iron-grey sky. If the van was going to make it up and down the hill several times, they'd have to work fast. Holly was already on the end of one of the bigger trees, with Saul at the other, and they were loading it into the back of the van. Laura and Emily stumped through the snow and fetched another.

'Hang on,' Laura said, dropping the trunk end and sending up an icy shower, 'how will people know to go to Mistletoe Cottage?'

'Ah.' Clayton rubbed his chin. 'We could change the notices?'

'No, we couldn't,' Saul said, coming up beside him.

'Leave this with me.' Emily produced her mobile phone from her coat pocket. She looked at Laura. 'I'll nip up to the house and make a couple of calls. It's perishing out here.'

'The back door's open. But what...?'

Emily was off, tramping purposefully up the drive.

Laura stoked up the fire in the living room, then held out her hands to warm them. Around the room sat Holly, Saul and Clayton. Mugs of tomato soup were clutched in freezing hands or stood on the coffee table, along with a plate of thick, buttered slices of crusty bread, and wedges of cheese. Saul was sitting on the floor in front of Holly's chair; he couldn't have got much closer to her unless he'd sat on her lap. Clayton was on the big sofa, legs stretched out in front of him. The sight of his socked feet seemed almost too intimate and Laura had to look away.

Emily came back from the kitchen with Laura's portable radio. She dropped onto the rug in front of the fire, setting the radio down beside her.

'Listen, it's on again.'

Clayton's face broke into a smile as they listened to the *Cuckmere Sounds* presenter announcing, for the third time in the last hour, the relocation of Charnley Acre's Christmas tree sales from Spindlewood to Mistletoe Cottage, Squirrel Lane.

'Amazing,' he said. 'I'm eternally grateful to you, Emily.'

She shrugged. 'What's the good of having contacts if you don't use them now and again?'

'I'm glad you said we won't be there till after two,' Saul said to Emily. 'I'm exhausted after humping trees about in the snow.'

Clayton shook his head and winked at Laura. 'The young have no stamina.'

'I can't imagine,' Laura said, 'why anyone would want to leave buying their tree until the day before Christmas Eve. I like plenty of time to enjoy mine.'

'Yes, but if you want to be traditional about it, Christmas Eve's the correct time to put the tree up,' Emily said.

'And take it down on Twelfth Night,' added Holly. 'We do

that bit, and then the house looks so bare for ages, without the lights and the sparkle.'

Laura glanced at Clayton to see how he was coping with the Christmassy chat. He met her gaze and held it for a long moment. '*I'm fine*,' his eyes seemed to say.

Laura gave a little nod, and smiled. Then, realising Holly had taken in this silent exchange and was gazing curiously at the pair of them, she busied herself with clearing away the soup mugs.

In the corner of the kitchen stood the hot chestnut brazier and the pan of leftover chestnuts, as well as rolls of twine and other rescued bits and pieces. The netting machine had gone in the van with the last of the trees. Turning round from the sink, Laura realised Clayton had come into the kitchen, silent on socked feet. He'd closed the door behind him.

'Laura, I don't know what I'd have done without you today – Holly and Emily, too, of course. You've been great over this whole tree thing, considering...'

He glanced down, clearly a little embarrassed.

'Considering I was in a relationship with Spencer Jennings. Or should I say, Marcus Dartnell?' she added softly. Clayton looked up in surprise. 'Yes, I know all about him and what happened,' Laura said. 'I know how Louise died, and I'm so very sorry, I can't begin to tell you how much.'

Her voice caught in her throat. She felt tears prick her lids. One squeezed its way out.

'Hey, no, Laura, please don't be upset.'

A second's hesitation, then Clayton was there, gathering her into a hug. They stood, holding one another, for what seemed like an age. When they parted, Clayton kept hold of her hand.

'I don't know how you found out – I can't imagine it was from Spencer – but you don't have to tell me. I just want to say that I'm glad you know, and I hope the two of you can work through it and be happy.'

Clayton's voice was gruff, full of emotion. Laura had to fight back the tears again.

'Clayton,' she said, 'I don't think you heard what I said, that I *was* with Spencer. That was then. Not now. He doesn't know that yet, but he soon will, once I've spoken to him.'

Clayton's brown eyes were intense, narrowed. 'You're letting him go because of what he did. Because of me?'

'Of course,' Laura said. 'What else would I do? Clayton, I care about you far too much to have stayed with Spencer, now that I know what happened. And it's not just that. I couldn't be with a man who kept that big a secret from me, forever hoping I'd never find out. How could I ever trust him over anything after that?'

The kitchen door opened. They sprung apart and Clayton let go of Laura's hand, but not before Saul had noticed, judging by the amused look on his face.

'I just came to say we should probably get going,' Saul said. 'It's only snowing a bit but it'll be icy on the hill, the colder it gets.'

'That's me told.' Clayton laughed, and, casting a private glance at Laura, fetched his boots from beside the back door.

CHAPTER 24

There'd been no more snow overnight. The morning began bitterly cold, but gradually a weak sun forced its way through the murky clouds and the temperature rose, sending flumps of snow crashing from the treetops and staining the higher areas of Spindlewood's undulating lawn seaweed green.

Watching from the turret, Laura couldn't help feeling disappointed that she wasn't going to have her white Christmas after all. But, thinking about Clayton at Mistletoe Cottage with his lovely trees, she was glad the conditions had improved. Besides, she didn't want people to miss out on her party because of the weather, and of course Mum and the rest of her family needed to make their journey safely, too, if they were all to spend Christmas together.

Yesterday afternoon she'd received a short text from Spencer saying he realised that she hadn't come over because of the snow, and he'd see her soon. Her first thought had been to wonder why he hadn't phoned instead of texting, but when she rang him soon after and heard the wariness in his voice, she realised he must have been worried after all about why she wanted to talk to him.

For a moment, she'd felt sympathy for him – an automatic reaction – after all, this was the man she'd been in love with. It had taken all her strength and nerve to contain her emotions as she'd told him, in a calm, factual way, of her recent discovery.

He'd hardly waited until she'd finished before he began to speak. Laura had cut him short. 'Spencer, just tell me if it's true. That's all I need you to say.'

There'd been a short, heavy silence. And then, predictably, he'd launched into his version of the story which he must have got off pat, having clearly told it a hundred times before. Laura had listened as patiently as she could, without interrupting.

'I don't have to ask what lies Clayton Masters has been feeding you,' Spencer said finally, with a hint of a sigh, 'but you really need to trust me on this. Louise Masters' death was not my fault, only certain people seemed to think it was fine to go against the court's ruling and pillory me for it.'

'It wasn't Clayton who told me about it. He's never said a word against you, as it happens.'

'Well, who did then?' Spencer had said belligerently.

Laura decided to ignore that. It was none of his business how she knew, and she certainly wasn't going to argue the toss about who was telling the truth and who was lying; it was pointless.

Instead, she'd said, 'You're using an assumed name and you know exactly who filled me in on that little deception.'

'Ah, yes, your "best friend". Some friend she must be to go around upsetting you for no reason.'

No reason?

'The point is, Spencer, you never told me. How was that ever going to work? So much for trust.'

'It was never important. I'm the same man, whatever I choose to call myself.'

'A man I thought I knew inside out.' Laura's stress levels had spiked at this point. 'Obviously, I was wrong.'

'Laura, names don't mean anything. They're just labels.'

'Why did you change yours, then?' she'd snapped back.

She hadn't given him the chance to answer; she would only have heard more excuses, more tales of woe. Instead, she said simply, 'I can't be with you anymore. It's over.'

And then his voice had softened as the protestations started. He loved her, they could have a good life together, she should look to the future, not the past; all that. And then he'd played his trump card. Except that it wasn't.

'Laura, listen, you remember I said we should make this Christmas Eve special?'

As if it wasn't already. 'Yes, so...'

'I was going to ask you to marry me, at the party.'

'What, in front of everyone?' She hadn't been able to stop herself from saying that, even though it was hardly relevant anymore.

'Yes. If you're going to do something, you should do it in style.'

Whose style? Certainly not hers. A vision of Spencer going down on one knee in a room full of partygoers had flung itself wildly into her brain. She'd have hated that, and the worst part – the saddest part – was that Spencer didn't know her well enough to understand that.

She wasn't sure she believed he'd planned to propose, anyway. It sounded suspiciously like a last attempt to win her over. But by that point, she was past caring whether it was true or not; she'd felt nothing except the pain of Spencer's betrayal.

And so, it was done. He'd tried to persuade her to let him come over so that they could talk properly.

'No. I'm sorry, Spencer, or whoever you are today. There's no point,' she'd said.

And then she'd cut off the call. Or maybe he had, she didn't know which, now.

Laura came away from the window and went to the shelves they'd had made especially to fit the curved walls of the turret room. Most of them were filled with books, but one held a collection of framed photos: a grinning James, up to his shins in nettles in the wilderness that had been their garden when they'd first moved here; the two of them arm in arm beneath the rose arch before it actually had any roses – her mother had taken that one; Holly on James's shoulders in a park; herself with Holly on a holiday beach... Her chest suddenly felt heavy, her breathing laboured, as she was overcome with sadness. She didn't want to cry – she refused to let the tears come, although at that moment she could have cried a lakeful of them.

Delayed reaction, she supposed.

Returning to the window, she gazed out at the garden, imagining how gloriously vibrant it would look in spring when the crocuses and daffodils, and then the tulips, were back. Later would come the dramatic sheaves of acid-green euphorbias, the showy, sugar-pink peonies, the stately gold-and-purple irises, and the creamy white nicotiana and lace-cap hydrangeas which seemed to glow in the fading evening light. There were so many good things to look forward to. Her sadness almost passed for now, Laura smiled.

CHAPTER 25

Holly was on a tour of inspection in the kitchen, opening and closing fridge, freezer and larder doors. It was a good thing the snow was melting, really, otherwise people wouldn't be able to get here for the Christmas Eve party, nor Nan and everyone else on Christmas Day, and then all this food – enough to feed the whole village for a week – would go to waste. Well, not all of it. Holly pinched a squidgy, dark-chocolate brownie from the plastic box in the larder and bit into it.

Through the window, she saw a robin perched on the wall. It cocked its head prettily to one side, then vanished with a flash of red into the tangle of the hedge. Looking at the garden, Holly was reminded of Clayton. The way he'd smiled at her mum the other day, all sort of secretively, like it was just the two of them and there was nobody else around, had got her thinking. She never normally liked to dwell too much on the topic of her mother's love life – well, you didn't, did you? – but it was glaringly obvious she liked Clayton, and not just for his gardening skills. And he *definitely* liked her. She was an attractive woman, still, of course. Why wouldn't he like her? Any decent bloke over a certain age would. And now Mum had dumped Spencer, who knew what might happen?

Holly finished her brownie and wiped her fingers on the tea-towel. That was a bit of a mystery, the split with Spencer. Her mum had said would Holly mind if she didn't tell her exactly what happened just yet because it was all a bit much, so it must have been over something quite serious, especially with it happening so close to Christmas. Holly couldn't say she was sorry, though.

Her thoughts turned to Lorcan. Now that she was seeing him every day at uni, she had the sneaking feeling that maybe, just maybe, she wasn't *quite* as much in love with him as she'd thought. It was too soon to tell, properly, though. Besides, she did love him enough to miss him like mad. They'd talked on the phone last night. Daft talk, lovey stuff, stuff that Holly couldn't have imagined herself saying in a million years, until she'd met Lorcan. But when he'd said he wished Christmas would get on and be over so they could be back at uni, Holly had thought, *no, that's wrong*. Christmas, with all its glitz and tackiness, was wonderful, and no matter how childish that was, she'd always think so, the same as her mum did, and Dad had too, although he'd never admitted it.

Come to think of it, where was Mum? Oh yes. Holly had passed her on the stairs earlier, going up to the turret. The turret was her mum's thinking place. Most likely she was up there now, thinking about rotten old Spencer. Holly hoped she wasn't brooding too much. If she didn't come down soon, she'd go up and see if she was all right.

Her mobile beeped and vibrated. She took it out of the pocket of her hoodie.

'Oh, hi, Saul!'

'Hi, Holly. Look, now the snow's clearing, how d'you fancy

meeting me in the village? We could... oh, I don't know, walk a bit, grab a bit of lunch in the Goose?'

'I thought you were at Clayton's house, selling Christmas trees?'

'Nope. We're nearly sold out and Clay said he can manage on his own, so I've got the day off.'

Holly thought for a moment. Really she should hang on here, make sure her mum was cool and everything, and not moping too much about Spencer. But in truth, she'd like to be out of doors, and she needed to check out the village to see if anything had changed since she was last home.

'Okay.'

They went to the Ginger Cat for lunch, Holly's choice. Saul would have preferred a private corner in the Goose and Feather or one of the other pubs, but as long as Holly was happy, that was all that mattered.

Before lunch, they'd walked all the way up the high street, looking at the Christmas displays in the shop windows, then crossed over and walked all the way back down the other side. Holly said she'd missed Charnley Acre when she was in Birmingham, and that she must've turned into a real country bumpkin. *The prettiest bumpkin he'd ever seen*, Saul had thought. But of course, he hadn't said it. He'd walked kind of close to her, so that it would be easy to catch her hand, but when he'd reached for it, she'd quickly put her hands in her pockets. He tried not to read anything bad into that, but it wasn't easy.

There was a live act on in the Goose tonight. A couple of guys with guitars. A bit folkish, but if you could get past that, they weren't at all bad. Saul planned to go but when he'd mentioned it to Holly earlier she said she'd promised to spend the evening at home with her mother, which sounded like an excuse to him. But then, she'd cheered him up no end by inviting him to the Christmas Eve party at her house. Actually, Laura had already invited him, but he accepted this second invitation like it was the first.

The soup bowls were empty and the bread eaten before Saul found the right moment to say what had been on his mind the whole time.

'After Christmas, I thought we could go into Brighton one night, have dinner, or see a film, if there's anything on you fancy?'

'Like, go on a proper date?'

'Yep, a date. I'd really like to take you out, Holly.'

The warm smile she gave him spoke of success. Then she leaned into the table, and her eyes had a serious look about them.

'Saul, I'm sorry but I can't go out with you, not like that. We can see each other around, like before, but I'm going out with somebody at uni and it wouldn't be right. Even if I wasn't seeing anyone... the distance, you know? It just wouldn't work.'

He didn't know why he was surprised. Except that night, in October... But hey, it was just a snog. Happened all the time, didn't it? Yep. *Get over it, Fielding*.

He nodded. He tried to smile but for some reason his face wasn't co-operating.

'Gotcha. No worries. It was just an idea, a spur-of-the-moment thing.'

She didn't believe that any more than he did, he could tell. There was a brief, slightly awkward silence, during which Saul realised he wasn't quite as devastated as he might be that Holly had knocked him back. A bit miserable, and hacked off, but not devastated. Odd, this love stuff, wasn't it? Had you fooled, if you didn't watch out.

Holly looked up brightly at him, as if she'd just remembered something.

'D'you think Clayton likes my mum? You know, *likes* her?' She pulled a face, as if she was talking about something distasteful.

Saul laughed. 'I'm damn sure he does. I reckon she's not exactly averse to him, either.'

'That's what I thought. She's finished with Spencer Jennings, you know.'

'Has she? Blimey, that was a bit sudden, wasn't it?'

'Yep.' Holly grinned.

'Interesting.'

'It could be.'

'Watch this space, then,' Saul said.

They left the Ginger Cat shortly afterwards. He walked with Holly to the bottom of Charnley Hill. He would have walked with her all the way to her house but it didn't seem the thing to do, under the circumstances. Saying goodbye felt a bit tricky, but they had a bit of a hug, mouths brushing against cheeks, and it was fine.

Instead of going straight home, Saul walked back to the village and ducked into the Goose. George was in the back room with another couple of mates, playing pool. Saul got himself a pint to drown his sorrows and joined in the game.

CHAPTER 26

Laura felt restless. Holly had been out – down to the village, she said – and come back, and then she'd taken a call on her mobile and gone out again, jumping into a car with three of her old friends from school. It was strange, but the house felt emptier now than when Holly was away in Birmingham.

On impulse, Laura snatched her duffle coat from the hook. Letting herself out of the back door, she rounded the corner of the house and set off down the drive, her hands in her pockets. The drive itself was clear now, but remnants of snow iced the tops of the bushes, and formed frozen, glittering heaps in the corners. It was almost four o'clock and the day was closing in. The sun was sinking below the distant hills, the denim-blue sky melting into streamers of turquoise and pink and apricot behind the dark skeletons of the trees. This was her favourite time of the day, in winter.

Silence ruled the garden. No birds, no traffic, no voices. Laura breathed deeply, and let the peacefulness envelop her.

Reaching the lower part of the drive, she saw that the abandoned awning which had covered the tree sales site now leaned drunkenly to one side on collapsing poles. Melted snow had formed a puddle on top. The boards were still down on the ground. They were slippery with icy water, and Laura trod carefully as she crossed them. She didn't know why she'd stopped off here, just that the site seemed sort of lonely, with all its trees and people gone. She spotted the branch of a Christmas tree, poking out from a pile of snow, as if it was waving for attention. Stooping, she tugged at it. Nothing happened at first, and then it shifted, the snow fell away, and a whole tree emerged, a small one, fairly intact with just a few of its branches bent. Laura smiled as she held the tree aloft by its trunk.

Clayton opened the door of Mistletoe Cottage and reeled back in astonishment.

'Yours, I believe,' Laura said, from behind the branches of a Christmas tree. 'I found it all alone in the snow. I'll bring it in, shall I?'

He stepped out of the door, about to take the tree from her and throw it onto the garden when she sidestepped him and marched straight into the house, tree and all. By the time he'd followed her in and closed the door, she was standing in the middle of his living room.

'Over there, I think?' She was looking towards the corner, by the back window, holding the tree in front of her with both hands. 'We'll need something to stand it in.'

'Laura, I don't...'

Clayton rubbed the top of his head. Emotions were crowding in – confused emotions – at the sight of Laura herself, and of a Christmas tree, right here, inside his house.

She gave him a long, enquiring look, and then her shoulders

drooped and she seemed to subside. The tatty little tree seemed to subside along with her.

'Oh God, I've got it wrong, haven't I? Clayton, I'm *so* sorry. I don't know what I was thinking. Well, I do, but I can see it's too soon.' She lowered the tree, her hands fumbling to maintain a grip on its spindly trunk. 'It's okay. I'll take this away right now and you can forget I ever came. I'm *so* sorry for interfering.'

Clayton took the tree out of Laura's hands. Her gloves were dirty; she had pine needles on the front of her coat and in her hair. The tip of her nose was pink from the cold. He'd never wanted to kiss her as much as he did now.

'Please stop saying sorry,' he said, 'otherwise I might have to put you out in the garden instead of this.' He stood the tree down, leaning it against the sofa. 'I've got a bucket. Will that do?'

Laura bit her lower lip, and nodded. Her eyes were shiny-wet, which might have been from the cold air outside. He thought not.

He went to fetch the bucket. Laura went back to her car and returned with a cardboard box full of decorations, including a set of multicoloured lights with most of the bulbs working. Half an hour later, with a combined effort, the little tree was steady in its bucket, decorated, and the lights plugged in and switched on. A slightly creased gold paper star crowned the top. Laura had even pulled a wad of red crepe paper out of the cardboard box and wrapped it round the bucket to disguise it.

They stood back to admire the tree. It had grown dark outside and the tree lights were sending a colourful glow around the walls. The only other light in the room came from the flames of the wood-burner and the lamp in the window. The tree lights became a rainbow blur as Clayton gazed at them. He blinked, and swallowed the lump in his throat.

'Are you all right?' Laura said softly.

He turned towards her. 'Yes, I'm all right. Well, perhaps not quite all right yet, but I will be. Thank you, Laura. For this. For, well, you know…'

She nodded. 'I'll go now and leave you in peace.' She picked up her coat from the arm of the chair. 'Clayton, I would very much like you to come to my party tomorrow, but at the same time I completely get it if you feel it's too much. I just want you to know that.'

'As it happens,' Clayton said, 'there's something I want you to know, too.'

And without waiting for Laura to ask what it was, he took a step towards her, placed his hands on her shoulders and kissed her.

CHAPTER 27

It was the day before Christmas Eve. Veronica wondered whether she should bother opening the shop. She hadn't in previous years; knitting wool and haberdashery wouldn't feature on anyone's list today, and she always closed on Christmas Eve. If anyone was in desperate need of safety pins or scissors, they could pick them up at the post office and general store. But she felt too restless to sit around indoors, and the hours would pass slowly.

Everything was ready for Christmas dinner, the day after tomorrow. Veronica liked to be organised. The turkey crown had been collected from the butchers, the vegetables and homemade Christmas pudding waited in the fridge and larder. She'd bought a frosted chocolate log, which Jack preferred to fruit cake, and the sausage rolls and mince pies were made. Tomorrow she would peel the vegetables and make a winter salad for Christmas tea. There were no other preparations she could make in advance.

It was a sunny day, bright and crisp, the sky a brilliant acidic blue. Jack had said he was going to the allotment, if she didn't mind – of course she didn't, as long as he was happy. He was in the kitchen now, humming to himself as he made a flask of tea to take with him. If Jack was going to be out, she may as well open the shop, at least for the morning. She could always close at lunchtime if it was quiet.

Her first customer of the day was Holly Engleby, Laura's daughter. Veronica asked her how she was getting on at university, and they had a chat about that while Holly browsed the shelves and display baskets.

'Have you got....?' Holly began, then turned to Veronica with a smile. 'Yep, here they are.'

'You're wanting embroidery kits? You do surprise me.' Veronica winked.

Holly laughed. 'Not for me. I wouldn't know one end of a needle from the other.'

'Well, one end has a little hole...' Veronica said, with mock seriousness.

'Yeah, right. No, it's for my nan. I haven't got her a pressie yet and Mum said she does cross-stitch and stuff so I thought one of these kits would do. I'm glad you're open, otherwise she'd have had to make do with chocs.' Holly sighed. 'My bad for not getting her something decent before.'

Veronica hid a smile. 'I'm sure she'd love a cross-stitch kit. Do you want me to help you choose?'

Holly stopped flicking through the packets on the stand. 'Cool. Thanks. I guess you're about the same age as Nan. Bit older, p'raps.'

Again, Veronica smothered a grin and came out from behind the counter. 'Come on, then. Let's see what there is.'

Ten minutes later, Holly left the shop with her purchases: one kit with a seaside scene to make into a small picture, and another with a modern floral design for a needle case.

Seeing Holly had reminded Veronica about the party up at

Spindlewood. Not that she had forgotten, but she had deliberately pushed it to the back of her mind.

She'd made one more evening trip to the pub, or rather, she'd intended to, but somehow it didn't happen. With Jack's approval – though not quite so willingly given as before, Veronica had noticed – she'd got herself ready and set off into the winter dark. She'd only got as far as the end of Mill Street where it met the high street when she'd stopped, wondering what on earth she thought she was playing at. She didn't fancy a drink, and casting herself adrift among a sea of other pubgoers, friendly or not, suddenly felt like too much effort. A cosy evening at home with Jack and the telly was much more appealing.

Telling herself she was being weak and stupid, Veronica carried on walking until she reached the Goose and Feather. The Christmas tree was up inside, its lights winking merrily through the bubble-glass window, and a string of fairy lights festooned the lintel above the door. The buzz of voices was just about audible as Veronica stood uncertainly in the doorway. No doubt she'd receive as warm a welcome as she had before. But wasn't there an equally warm welcome, and a much more meaningful one, waiting for her in the cottage?

Veronica had turned around and gone straight back home.

Jack looked up from his armchair in surprise.

'Back already? What happened? Pub burned down has it?' He chuckled. 'Or did you forget your purse?'

His blue eyes were all wrinkly at the corners, always a sign he was really pleased about something.

Veronica had taken her coat off and, leaving it on the back of a dining chair, sat down on the sofa. 'Nope. The pub's still standing and I didn't forget anything, either.' She paused, meeting Jack's gaze with her own. 'Except maybe I forgot how lucky I am to have you and our lovely home. Can't get enough of it. Or you, if you must know.'

There'd been a small silence. And then the lights on the Christmas tree suddenly took on a life of their own and started a hectic round of chasing.

Jack had looked at the dazzling display. 'Don't know what's got into the damn lights. Maybe we should have bought some new ones. The settings keep changing by themselves. I'll have to fix that.'

'Not now. Stay still,' Veronica had said. 'They'll change again in a minute. Look, Jack...' She'd stopped, not knowing what she'd been going to say, or what she *could* say. The right words were suddenly very far away.

'Love, it's okay. I get it.' Jack had rubbed the side of his face. 'I know I've not been much fun, not for ages now. I get all churned up inside whenever I think I should be doing something, going somewhere. It feels kind of safer, somehow, stopping here, going down the allotment, not doing a lot else. Don't ask me why because I don't know. But you, you're different. You need people, you need to be where there's something happening now and again, I realise that, and I'd never stop you. I wouldn't do that.'

'I know,' Veronica had said quietly. Tears had formed behind her eyes. 'I know, Jack, and whatever it is you want, I want it too. Yes, perhaps I'd like us to do something different for a change, go places – together, not just me. I do think that sometimes. But it's only ever a passing thought, so don't you worry about that. As I said, as long as I've got you and our little home, that's well enough for me.'

'And the shop. Don't forget the shop.'

'And the shop, yes. I love my little shop.'

And my little world, she was thinking, as Jack raised himself out of his chair, came over and planted a warm kiss on her cheek. She'd pulled him to her so that he'd sat down on the sofa with a bump, her arms still around him. Then she'd kissed him too, a fleeting, tender kiss on his lips.

'What was that for?' He'd laughed.

'Oh, just for being you,' she'd said.

Jack had shaken his head. 'You're daft, you are.' He'd wriggled out of her arms. 'I'll make the hot chocolate. Or, how about we open one of the bottles of wine we got in for Christmas?'

He'd been up and fetching the glasses from the sideboard before she could reply.

Veronica went into the back room of the shop, made a mug of coffee and brought it back through. She sipped it pensively as she gazed out at Charnley Acre's high street, at the shops with their festive window displays, the people bustling by on their pre-Christmas errands, the stuttering stream of traffic. Her village – *their* village. Home. There was nowhere better.

Then the shop door tinkled and a woman she knew by sight ducked under the low lintel of the doorway and came up to the counter. She wanted yellow baby wool and a pattern. Her daughter had just announced her pregnancy and the grandmother-to-be couldn't wait to start on the baby's wardrobe. Veronica was pleased to oblige. She'd long ago expected the knitting of baby clothes to fade out; there were such lovely clothes for kiddies in the big shops, and cheap, too. But plenty of new mums favoured the traditional, and hand-knitting had taken an upward turn.

Veronica offered her best wishes as the woman left. Two more customers came in after her, and then the street outside fell quiet, as did the shop. It was almost midday, and she thought she may as well close up.

She was just putting everything straight on the counter when the door opened and Jack ducked inside. Veronica smiled in surprise. She noticed he'd changed out of the old cord trousers and jacket he wore to the allotment and was wearing his navy chinos with his dark-grey bomber jacket.

'I wasn't expecting you,' Veronica said, unnecessarily. 'I was about to shut up shop. You can walk me home. That'll be nice.'

'I could. I've got a question to ask you first.'

Veronica frowned. 'What question?'

Jack came right up to the counter and leaned both hands on it. 'This party. Christmas Eve. Mrs Engleby's place...'

'Laura's, yes. What about it?' Veronica had already made up her mind she wasn't going to mention the party again. She'd be going up to Spindlewood tomorrow evening. It was such a lovely occasion and she couldn't miss it. But she wouldn't ask Jack if he'd go with her, not anymore. She would simply respect his wishes and let him be.

'What're you wearing? To the party?'

Veronica laughed. 'Why are you interested in what I'm wearing? My usual, I expect. My dark-green velvet dress. Why?'

'And you'll look lovely in it, as you always do. But how about something new? A brand-new dress that'll make you the belle of the ball?'

Veronica's mouth fell open. She didn't need a new dress for the party. The green velvet fitted her still trim figure, and suited the occasion.

'Jack, it's the day before Christmas Eve! Even if I needed a dress, which I don't, there's nowhere in the village to get one and it's too late to order online. Let me lock up and we'll go home for lunch.'

But Jack was shaking his head. 'Not an option. There'll be clothes shops open in Cliffhaven. Not many, I grant you, but I bet you we'll find something. We can grab a bite of lunch while we're down there.' He threw up his hands and grinned. 'Who says I can't be spontaneous?'

Veronica had to laugh. In fact, she burst into a fit of uncontrolled giggles.

'And while we're down there I might treat myself to a new shirt. For the party.' Jack's face had turned a bit pink.

'You're coming to the party? The Spindlewood party?' she asked, hardly able to get the words out.

'That's what I said, didn't I? Someone's gotta keep an eye on you. Get your coat, woman. The next bus is in eight minutes. We'll have to hurry. We don't want to be getting down there after dark.'

CHAPTER 28

Laura left the house and sauntered down Charnley Hill to the village. Christmas Eve had finally arrived and the high street was busy with people doing last-minute shopping, enjoying a well-deserved break at the Ginger Cat Café, or, like Laura herself, just out for some air and a change of scene.

Veronica came out of the café as Laura was passing by.

'Jack's popped up the allotment to cut us a cabbage for tomorrow so I thought I'd treat myself to coffee and a bun.' She placed a hand on Laura's arm. 'Lovely to see you. Everything ready for tonight?'

'More or less. There's bound to be something I've forgotten but whatever it is, it won't be missed. There should be a good crowd. Most people accepted and those that didn't will probably turn up anyway.'

'They will indeed. And is Cynthia ready to party?'

'She most definitely is, now she's all glammed up in pink.'

Veronica smiled, tilting her head to one side. 'Well, I shall be in competition with Cynthia this year. I've got a new dress! Red, it is, with long sleeves and quite a low neckline. More glam than the green velvet I usually turn up in but it is a party, and red's such a Christmassy colour.'

'Sounds gorgeous,' Laura said. 'It gives you a lift, having something new to wear, doesn't it?'

'It does.' Veronica nodded vigorously, her expression lively in a way that piqued Laura's curiosity. 'Jack bought it for me as a surprise. Well, I was with him, of course. He whisked me down to Cliffhaven yesterday afternoon, all of a sudden. I found it in that little boutique just off the main square. And then we made it to the men's shop just before it shut, and Jack bought a smart blue shirt, so we'll both be in our glad rags tonight.'

'Both? Jack's coming to the party?' Laura was astonished, and delighted. 'That's...'

'I know! I'm as surprised as you are. It's a real turn up for the books. Well, I'd better get home.' Veronica stepped towards the kerb, then added, as if it was an afterthought, 'I'm glad all that dreadful business over the development site's out of the way. The new houses will be up before we know it, and everyone will have forgotten they ever made a fuss in the first place.'

Veronica was obviously fishing for a bit of gossip, although sweet as she was, she'd never come right out and ask a direct question.

Laura just nodded. Veronica looked a little disappointed at the lack of reaction, but clearly the topic was still on her mind.

'Yes, I did think about sending Jack up to your place to get one of Mr Masters' lovely trees, but in the end I got the old one out of the attic. It's artificial but you don't get needles in the carpet.'

'Whereas I shall be sweeping them up forever more.'

Laura left Veronica waiting by the kerb for a gap in the traffic and continued her stroll along the street. A little further on, she passed Veronica's wool shop. A felt-tipped notice was fixed to the inside of the door: *Wishing all my customers a very Happy Christmas. Shop closed until New Year.*

There were similar notices appearing on shop doors and windows as Laura made her way along the high street. Everyone was anxious to start their Christmas festivities, and who could blame them?

Stopping outside the bakery displaying one lonely loaf and four mince pies in the window, Laura took out her phone and dashed off a quick text to Emily, asking if she was at home and receiving visitors. The answer came back immediately: *Yes! Come now.*

Laura thought for a moment before she texted back: *Have to stop off somewhere first. Won't be long.*

Smartening her steps, she reached the lych-gate of St Luke's and passed through. The heavy oak door of the church was closed but not locked. Laura lifted and twisted the black iron handle and went in. At four o'clock this afternoon there would be a crib service for the children, and tonight, the usual gathering for midnight mass, but now the church was deserted. Laura heard her own footsteps echoing on the ancient stone floor as she wandered down one of the side aisles. Along the length of the aisle, plump, waxy candles flickered in carved stone niches, decked with greenery and studded with bright holly berries. The candles weren't real – they'd stopped leaving real ones alight – but they were no less beautiful for that. The real candles, those in the silver holders on the altar, would be lit tonight, when organ music and the sweet sound of carols would rise gloriously to the rafters.

She and James had attended midnight mass a few times over the years, and then the party had taken over and somehow, not surprisingly, they'd stopped. Some of Laura's guests tonight would come to mass, though, leaving the party in time to process down the hill and through the village to the church.

James's funeral service had been held at St Luke's, although he wasn't buried in the churchyard. He hadn't been a believer, but Laura had felt comforted in the traditional, familiar setting with her favourite hymns as part of the service, and she was sure James would not have minded.

At the end of the aisle, she turned to the centre and stood facing the altar with its magnificent display of winter flowers and silvered greenery, and above, the beautiful stained-glass window depicting Luke, the physician, tending to the sick. She said a silent prayer for James, then turned and walked back down the carpeted central aisle. A movement caught her eye and the verger, a short, squarely-built woman appropriately named Mary, approached from the shadows at the side of the church.

'Hello, Laura.' She smiled. 'I saw you come in but I didn't want to disturb.'

'You wouldn't have been.' Laura smiled back. 'I just popped in to offer up a quick prayer for James.'

'Lovely,' Mary said, beaming. 'Busy day for you, I expect.'

'Yes, but perhaps not as busy as yours.' They both laughed. 'I like to make the time, if I can. I might not show my face here very often but, you know, I love this church. Not just for the religious side but because I like to think of all those feet traipsing through this same building for hundreds of years, and yet it's still here in Charnley Acre, like a solid, dependable heart that never stops beating.'

'My, that's poetic,' Mary said.

'Ha, yes, well it is Christmas. I think it does something to my brain cells. Seriously, though, I don't know how St Luke's is still standing, with all the troubles it's had.' She nodded towards a table by the door where several boxes with slots in the top were set out, each with a particular fund mentioned on the label.

Mary followed her line of sight. 'Between you and me, we've done a deal on the woodworm in the bell tower. One of the parishioners has connections with a good firm who said they'd give us a discount, so we're almost there on that one. And people are so kind, offering to give up their free time to come in and fix up this and that. He's one of them, that gardener fellow. What's his name?' Mary put a finger to her chin. 'Clayton, that's it.'

'*Clayton*? Really?' She shouldn't have been surprised, knowing what sort of man he was. 'What's he going to be doing?'

'Mm, not sure. Vicar knows. They were in a huddle the other day, discussing what he could do, I suppose. Like I say, people are so kind.'

Laura smiled. 'He offered to do some work on my house – Spindlewood. I think I may take him up on that. I'd pay him, of course.'

Mary clasped her hands across her expansive bosom. 'Ah yes, Spindlewood. Lovely house, and so well worth preserving. You're lucky to live there, Laura. You keep it going. It'll bring its own rewards. There's not much that can't be fixed up with some filler, a bit of new timber and a lot of faith, in my opinion.'

'You're absolutely right, Mary. And I fully intend to keep Spindlewood in one piece as long as I can still get up a ladder.'

'Hmm, I'd let him do the dangerous work. Clayton. Snap his hand off while the offer's still there, I would.'

Laura laughed. 'I might just do that.'

Halfway along the gravel path leading to the lych-gate, Laura stopped, quite suddenly, and turned to look back at the mellow stone walls of the church. What had she been thinking? She couldn't sell Spindlewood, not now. Probably not ever. It should be Holly's one day. Her daughter loved the house as much as she did, that was obvious every time she came home. Anyway, what did a few draughts and a drop of rainwater matter? The repairs could all be done gradually, and no doubt when they were done it would be time to start all over again, but that was fine. Besides, having had so much space for so long, she couldn't imagine living anywhere smaller, or away from Charnley Acre, and cottages of the kind she liked hardly ever came on the market anyway. Nor could she imagine herself in a cramped new-build, like the houses Spencer was putting up, although of course she'd manage if she had to.

'You're spoilt, do you know that?' Laura admonished herself, as she reached the lych-gate and left the churchyard.

But somebody had to be Spindlewood's guardian, and it may as well be her rather than some stranger who may not love it as much as she did.

Eight minutes later, Laura rang the bell at Cloud Cottage.

'You're puffed out,' Emily said, holding the door back to let her in. 'You're out of condition, that's your trouble.'

'Ta. Any coffee going?'

'I can do better than that.' Emily disappeared and came back with a bottle containing something red and glowing. 'Sloe gin. Dad makes it. This'll warm the cockles, and it is Christmas. I'm ever so glad you're here but what're you doing out anyway? Why aren't you up to your armpits in pastry and whatnot?'

Laura shrugged her coat off and sank onto Emily's sofa. 'It's all done. Well, that's not quite true but Holly's baking the sausage rolls and things that were in the freezer so I escaped. Wow, this is gorgeous!' She held up her little glass of sloe gin and gazed at the pretty ruby liquid. 'It's reaching parts I didn't know I had!'

'It does that.' Emily sat down in the armchair. Wilf ambled into the room and slumped on the carpet by her feet.

'I've just been to the church,' Laura said.

'For James?'

Laura nodded. 'James, yes. But while I was there I came to a decision.'

'Oh?'

'Yes. I'm not going to sell the house.'

Emily made a disappointed face. 'Of course you're not. I've always known that. I thought it was going to be something juicy.'

'Have you? I haven't. Anyway, sorry to let the side down but there's nothing juicy to tell.'

Except that Clayton kissed me. Laura fidgeted on the sofa and sipped some more sloe gin. One part of her longed to pass on this new information, analyse it and giggle over it with her friend. The other part of her, the part that was still reeling from that kiss, spoke more sense. It was too soon. Besides, it might never happen again; they'd both been feeling emotional at the time.

The Christmas tree she'd rescued from the snow and taken to Mistletoe Cottage had its work cut out. Firstly, it had to lead Clayton into believing that bad memories didn't have to ruin every one of his Christmases forever more, and then it had to help him put the Spencer business behind him and begin a proper recovery from Louise's death.

One wonky little Christmas tree with one heck of a task ahead of it. It was strange, but Laura preferred to think of it that way rather than give herself any credit for lifting some of Clayton's sadness. She may have given him a little nudge towards the light, but she wasn't a psychologist – or the Christmas fairy; she'd leave that privilege with Cynthia.

So, then, the kiss. Gratitude? A sudden rush of in-the-moment friendly affection? If there was nothing more to it than that, it was probably for the best. And wasn't that one depressing thought...

'Laura?'

Emily was looking quizzically at her. Laura realised she was smiling. She rallied, holding up her almost empty glass and squinting at the drop that remained. 'Blimey. If I'd known I'd be drinking this early I would have had a proper breakfast.'

'Sloe gin's not drinking. It's essential fortification for the partying to come. Pass that over and I'll give you a top-up.'

Laura clutched her glass. 'No more. I'll only drop off this afternoon and I haven't got time for that.'

Emily put the bottle down and narrowed her eyes. 'Laura, will you be okay tonight?'

She didn't have to explain further; she meant would Laura be okay without Spencer by her side at the party. She admitted she'd had a little wobble about that this morning. It would feel strange, and there were bound to be whispered comments and knowing looks amongst her guests. Nothing intentionally rude or unkind; it was just human nature, and the wobble had soon passed.

'Of course,' she said. 'I'll have you and Holly there, and anyway I'll be enjoying myself too much to notice.'

And who else might she have there? She gave herself no more than a second to dwell on that.

'It's a shame none of your dates worked out, Em.'

'Well, cheers! You make it sound as if that's it, game over!' Emily widened her eyes, and downed the rest of her sloe gin.

'You know I didn't mean it like that. I meant in time for Christmas, that's all.'

'Yeah, I know, me too. But there's a bright side. It leaves me free to flirt like merry hell with all the single blokes at your party.'

Laura giggled. 'You are joking. At the moment I can't even

think of a single guy I've invited. Not one that would suit you, anyway.'

'Yep, I'm joking. But come New Year, who knows? I might have struck lucky by then. The internet's like The Windmill Theatre.' Emily drew inverted commas in the air. 'We never close.'

CHAPTER 29

Spencer drove along Charnley Acre's high street, then, instead of heading for the main road out of the village, he took the turning at the crossroads that led up Charnley Hill. Snow was still banked up on either side, lumps of it, solid, dirty-looking, but the road was clear and ice-free. Just as well the temperature had switched up a few degrees, considering the long journey ahead of him.

The car slowed almost of its own accord as he reached the gates of Spindlewood. He wasn't sure what he was doing here. Tormenting himself wasn't something he was prone to. He'd never seen the point of dwelling on what might have been. And yet, here he was. He pulled the car slightly off the road and, parking it half on and half off the snow-strewn grass verge, killed the engine and got out of the car.

The hedge running along the front of the garden was shoulder high, and quite thick despite the winter leaf drop. But now he was here, he wanted more than a peek through the hedge. So what if he was seen? He hardly cared now. Stepping sideways, he ventured as far as the open gates and planted himself between them. From here he had an almost uninterrupted view of the garden and the house at the top of it.

The first thing that caught his eye was the flat area of lawn to the right of the path where it met the shrubbery. The grass was all churned up and deeply ridged in places. Until the snow disguised it, it must have been a sea of mud. He'd told Laura her garden would be wrecked by that man's temporary shop. He'd told her, and he'd been right, but she hadn't listened. Hadn't cared, more like. Oh yes, Laura's priorities had lain elsewhere, somewhere more telling than the state of her garden. No doubt about it.

At the thought of Clayton Masters and his pathetic whinging about the accident, his outburst in court and the lies he'd spread in order to place the blame for his sister's death firmly at Spencer's feet, he felt heat rising through his body, despite the coldness of the day.

The heat of anger and frustration and... something else. What was that? Regret? Guilt?

Regret that the episode on that country road at night had happened in the first place, certainly. Of course he regretted it, even though he hadn't been at fault, not for the girl's death, anyway; the court had ruled on that. Spencer believed in the strength of the British justice system, if he believed in anything. Common sense had prevailed, as well as lack of evidence to refute Spencer's account of the incident. Nobody could argue with that.

And yet they had. Or at least, one person had. More than one now, of course. He'd never had Laura down as a woman who was easily swayed – look how long it had taken him to lure her into bed. But he'd bet his last quid she was a fully paid up member of Team Masters now.

That was something else Spencer regretted: his abject failure to keep Laura and Clayton apart and the history between him and Masters under wraps. Failure wasn't part of his vocabulary. Or it hadn't been, before. He'd have to watch that in future.

Guilt? Was he feeling that, too? If so, the feeling came as an unwelcome surprise. Spencer gazed at the now empty space where the feet of half the village had so recently trod and, for once, thought about what it must be like to lose somebody close, so suddenly and unexpectedly. Somebody so young. He supposed he was lucky he'd never had to find out. The deaths of his grandparents, and a couple of old aunts and uncles had been sad, but even he realised that was hardly the same thing.

Louise, her name was. A lovely girl, the newspaper reports said. Kind, always thinking of others. Mind you, didn't they always say that? Yes, there was a certain amount of guilt there. Inside Spencer's brain, the word 'Sorry' slowly formed, as if he'd spoken it aloud. Maybe he did have a heart, after all.

Enough of the introspection. Spencer pulled his cashmere scarf up around his ears, thrust his hands deep inside his pockets and turned his gaze on the house. It was far too big for one person, anyone could see that. She was attached to the place purely for sentimental reasons, that had been clear from the start. Her husband – John? James? – had instigated its purchase; she'd once told him that. The first time Spencer had set eyes on Spindlewood, when he'd followed her home to make sure she arrived safely – a genuine reason, it really was – the house had spoken to him. He'd encountered hundreds of great houses, original one-offs that had delighted his eye and spilt pound signs into the air, but Spindlewood was the best of them. That turret with its fairy-tale appearance was the stuff of dreams. It leaked, of course, needed big bucks spent on it, like other parts of the house. But it was all fixable, and as he'd wandered around inside on his first visit, he'd calculated the space and reckoned he could make four apartments out of it, or maybe three and a couple of studios. The apartment with the turret would have been the star of the show, the most desirable. The most expensive.

Spencer had almost salivated as he'd envisaged the enticing sales brochure.

She would have gone for it, in the end. She could have had one of the apartments, the turret one, if she'd liked. Or she could have bought herself a little cottage in the village and had a nice little sum in the bank to boot. Yes, she would have seen the sense in selling him the place, eventually. Teachers didn't earn big money, and she didn't have a great deal to fall back on. One glance at her orderly files in the bedroom drawer had confirmed that.

Spencer stepped to one side and leaned on the gatepost, his thoughts coming from a different angle. Had he been going to ask Laura to marry him? Had he really, or had he said it in a last-ditch attempt to stop her from leaving him? Again, Spencer questioned his own feelings that seemed intent on scuppering his normal pragmatism today. Okay, he'd had feelings for her. She was a beauty, in an unassuming way he liked. She was thoughtful and amusing, and as enthusiastic about their lovemaking as he could have wished. Yes, Laura was great, and if it wasn't love he'd felt for her – he wasn't sure he even knew what that was – it must have been close. Close enough.

But marriage? If by any remote chance she'd have gone for it, he'd have found a way to back down afterwards. His feelings didn't extend quite that far. No, what he'd really wanted was to move into Spindlewood with her, enjoy all the fruits of the relationship while the subject of the house's development brewed nicely in the background.

But there, it wasn't to be. Things had a way of working out for the best in the end.

He'd briefly considered leaving Charnley Acre, once his plans had blown up in his face. In fact, he was still thinking it might be in his best interests to start afresh, somewhere new. But he liked the area; that was why he'd returned in the first place. And now he had even more business connections in Sussex than before, and good people working for him, too. Shame to waste all that. He was even set to recoup the outlay on that site with the Japanese knotweed. The horrible, costly stuff was no more.

Spencer shivered. It was only late morning but the sky above the chimneys of Spindlewood had darkened while he'd been standing here. Perhaps they were in for more snow. Just then, a light went on in the turret, joining the others in the downstairs rooms. In some of the rooms, even from this distance, he detected glitter and sparkle. Along the frontage of the house, fairy lights bobbed and swayed, and there were coloured lights strung across the bushes nearest the house.

The party. Of course, it was Christmas Eve. He'd forgotten about the party. Tonight, the lovely Mrs Engleby would be playing hostess, and getting a thrill out of it. He could have been by her side, welcoming half the bloody village, wining and dining and entertaining them. She would have rewarded him amply later, he'd have been sure of that. He might even have wrangled an invitation to stay over and spend Christmas Day with her and her family. Instead, he'd be spending it at the old homestead with his parents, and possibly his brother, sister-in-law, and their kids. His parents were always on top form – no sign of the frailty he'd hinted at to Laura. At least they'd be pleased to see him.

Taking a last look at Spindlewood, Spencer returned to the car, stepped in and started up. Then, making a tight three-point turn, he drove back down Charnley Hill to begin the journey to Gloucestershire.

CHAPTER 30

Spindlewood looked wonderful, inside and out. Since darkness had fallen, the outdoor lights transformed the frosted garden into a magical winter fairyland. The lighted windows of the house with their sills full of greenery and sparkle gave the cheeriest of welcomes. Indoors, everywhere was warmth and colour and light. Everyone had pronounced the Christmas tree in the hall the 'best ever'. Cynthia in her new pink outfit drew plenty of compliments to which she responded with a beatific, plastic smile.

Laura roamed the downstairs rooms, chatting as she went. She was sure she didn't know all of these people, but no matter; the invitations to her Christmas Eve party were loose affairs, and the 'plus one' was liberally interpreted. As long as everyone enjoyed themselves – they certainly seemed to be doing so – she was happy.

The food which had filled the extended dining table, plus a range of small tables dotted around it, was nicely depleted, but there was still plenty left for latecomers and second rounds. In the background, Christmas songs played softly but they were no competition for the beat of the music coming from the living room where Holly was in charge of the playlist. From the doorway, Laura watched her daughter throw her head back in laughter at something one of her friends had said, then a whole bunch of them burst into raucous laughter, including Saul.

Holly had talked a little about Saul to Laura in the kitchen before the guests had arrived. She was obviously feeling guilty about him, but at the same time there was some confusion in her mind.

'What if I do really like Saul after all? I mean *properly* like him,' she'd said, launching herself on top of the kitchen counter and sitting cross-legged, like an elf.

'You can't mess him about, Hol,' Laura had said. 'Blowing hot one minute and cold the next.'

'Yeah, I know that.' She sighed. 'He is dead cute, though, isn't he?'

Laura had laughed. 'It takes a lot more than just being *cute*, Holly. Although Saul does have plenty of other good qualities, I'll give you that. Anyway, what about Lorcan? I thought the pair of you had sworn undying love?'

Laura had winked, causing Holly to scowl good-naturedly. Then she'd tossed her blonde hair back.

'Yes, well, I might have a little rethink on that.'

Laura had simply lifted her eyes to the ceiling in mock despair and gone to the fridge to take out the butter.

Holly and the younger set were dancing now, and then somebody switched the music from that awful beat stuff Holly liked to something more popular, and others began to join in the dancing, filling the space between the pushed-back sofas. Saul had been standing on one spot, his eyes never leaving Holly. And now Holly was going to him, taking his hand, drawing him in to dance with her.

Laura smiled, slowly shaking her head.

'What're you smiling at?' Emily was by Laura's side.

'Oh, just Holly. She doesn't seem to know what she wants where the boys are concerned.'

'And we did, at her age?'

'Fair point.'

Emily nudged Laura in the ribs. 'Look, see that guy in the blue shirt, the tall fair-haired one, over there?'

She waved a vague arm towards the far side of the room. Laura squinted through the dim lighting and the mass of people.

'I think so. Why?'

'He's the new doctor at Charnley Health Centre. He's just moved into the village. Cute, isn't he?'

Cute, again! Was there no other word to describe a good-looking man anymore? Laura peered once more into the gloom just as the crowd parted for a moment, giving her a better view.

'Wow. I see what you mean. I had no idea he was coming, but what's new?' She giggled.

Laura didn't remember inviting any doctors, but she had invited Sophie, one of the receptionists she'd been friendly with for ages. Which probably explained the number of other guests she'd recognised from the health centre.

'We've been chatting,' Emily continued, 'and how's this for coincidence? It turns out he's got a whippet, just out of puppyhood. I was explaining where the best walks are around the village.'

And no doubt imparting the full details of Wilf's walking routine on any given day of the week, Laura thought, smiling to herself. 'What else has he got besides the whippet? Wife? Girlfriend? Mistress?'

'Not the first two, as far as I can make out. The last one?' Emily shrugged, pulling a face. 'Who knows?'

They both burst into giggles.

Leaving Emily to weave her way back towards the

unsuspecting man of her latest dreams, Laura went to the kitchen, poured herself half a glass of wine and drank a little. Putting the glass down, she rested her hands on the cold edge of the sink and stared out at the black night through the uncurtained window, enjoying a moment of peace and quiet. And then, out of nowhere, came an odd sensation, as sudden as if she'd been nudged in the ribs. It felt almost like loss, as if she was missing something – or someone. It wasn't about James; she missed him every day and always would, but that was a different sort of feeling, one she'd grown so accustomed to that it was written into every cell of her being. Could this be about Spencer, then? Strange, if it was.

But perhaps it wasn't so strange. If you'd been in love with someone, however misguided, a little bit of the feeling must cling on for a while, like a strand of seaweed to a rock before the sea came and swept it away.

Goodness, that was a bit airy-fairy, even for her. Did it mean she'd drunk too much, or not enough? Laura lifted her glass, peered at its contents and topped it up from the bottle on the counter.

'Cheers!' she said to the empty kitchen. 'Happy Christmas!' Then, 'Chin-chin!' That had been one of James's sayings. She smiled at the memory.

She stayed in the kitchen for a while, sipping her wine and listening to the sounds of her guests filling Spindlewood with laughter and merriment. And then she thought about Mistletoe Cottage, its doors and curtains closed against the world, the little Christmas tree bravely lighting a silent room, and her heart twisted.

It was time she went back to her guests but another few minutes wouldn't hurt. Leaving the kitchen, Laura slipped along the hallway and went upstairs, taking the smaller staircase to the turret. She'd left the light on earlier; she switched it off now. As she stood at the window, gazing at the crescent moon suspended above the trees and the star-strewn clear winter sky, she sensed movement below. She looked down, and there was Clayton, walking up the drive, a note of uncertainty in his stride.

The turret room was dark but he must have sensed her presence because he stopped as he approached the steps to the terrace and looked up. His face broke into a smile. Laura smiled back. She lifted her hand as if to wave, but instead pressed it to the glass, fingers spread. Clayton raised his hand, mirroring hers. Then he began to walk up the steps and Laura ran down to let him in.

ACKNOWLEDGEMENTS

Firstly, a big thank you to Rachel Tyrer for taking me on as a new writer, to Tara Lyons for her excellent communication and guidance, and to all the lovely people at Bloodhound for presenting this first book in my Charnley Acre series so efficiently, and beautifully.

Special thanks also to my lovely family - Michael, Christopher, Luke and Stuart - and to my loyal band of friends, writerly and otherwise, who take such an interest in my writing and cheer me on all the way. I couldn't be doing this without you all!

A NOTE FROM THE PUBLISHER

Thank you for reading this book. If you enjoyed it please do consider leaving a review on Amazon to help others find it too.

We hate typos. All of our books have been rigorously edited and proofread, but sometimes mistakes do slip through. If you have spotted a typo, please do let us know and we can get it amended within hours.

info@bloodhoundbooks.com

Printed in Great Britain
by Amazon